"This might help me remember." His warm breath hit against her lips when he spoke.

And suddenly more than anything, Lenora wanted him to remember. Oh, and she wanted him to kiss her, too. Clayton might not have any memories of their one-night stand, but Lenora was well aware that he could set fires with his mouth.

He moved in closer. Closer. And she was just a breath away from kissing him again. Too bad she could already feel it and also too bad her body seemed to think this was foreplay, that Clayton would haul her off to bed again.

That wouldn't happen.

Even if she desperately wanted it.

Her eyelids were already fluttering down, getting ready for that kiss, when Clayton stopped. It took her a moment to realize why. The baby was kicking, and with her body pressed against Clayton's, he could feel it.

USA TODAY Bestselling Author

DELORES FOSSEN

ONE NIGHT STANDOFF

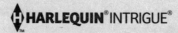
HARLEQUIN® INTRIGUE®

Recycling programs
for this product may
not exist in your area.

ISBN-13: 978-0-373-69692-5

ONE NIGHT STANDOFF

Printed in U.S.A.

ABOUT THE AUTHOR

Imagine a family tree that includes Texas cowboys, Choctaw and Cherokee Indians, a Louisiana pirate and a Scottish rebel who battled side by side with William Wallace. With ancestors like that, it's easy to understand why *USA TODAY* bestselling author and former air force captain Delores Fossen feels as if she were genetically predisposed to writing romances. Along the way to fulfilling her DNA destiny, Delores married an air force top gun who just happens to be of Viking descent. With all those romantic bases covered, she doesn't have to look too far for inspiration.

Books by Delores Fossen

CAST OF CHARACTERS

Marshal Clayton Caldwell—He must rely on broken memories and a mysterious woman, Lenora, to stay alive and outsmart a hired gun. Even though he'll protect her with his life, he's not sure he can trust her with his heart.

Lenora Whitaker—After a one-night stand with Clayton, Lenora realizes she's pregnant. However, her secret past is catching up with her, and it puts Clayton, their baby and her in the crosshairs of a killer.

Kirby Granger—Clayton's foster father who's under investigation for an old murder.

Adam Riggs—He's in jail awaiting trial for killing Lenora's friend, but he could have hired assassins to take out Clayton and Lenora so they can't testify against him.

James Britt—A Justice Department agent investigating the attempts to kill Lenora and Clayton, but he could have his own agenda.

Quentin Hewitt—Lenora's former boss and a man she once thought she loved. He could have strong objections to Lenora's involvement with Clayton.

Melvin Larson—Clayton's biological father. He abandoned Clayton years ago but now he's back.

Chapter One

Marshal Clayton Caldwell figured this could be *bad*.

He waited at the window and watched the woman exit the dark blue car that she'd just parked next to the Marshals Service building where he worked. She glanced around, but because of the other vehicles, there was no way she could have seen the black truck that eased to a stop about a half block up the street.

Clayton saw it, all right.

And he didn't like the looks of this.

Had the driver of the truck followed her?

And if so, why?

Since Clayton had been at the second-floor window finishing his morning coffee and watching for his visitor to arrive, he'd been able to see the car and truck. Both unfamiliar. Not that he knew every vehicle in Maverick Springs, but the truck's front license plate was obscured with mud or something. That, and the fact that the driver didn't get out, made Clayton very uneasy.

Or maybe that was just a reaction to Lenora Whitaker's visit.

Until the night before, he hadn't heard from her since—well, just *since*. After nearly two months, Clayton had figured it'd stay that way.

"Everything okay?" Harlan McKinney asked. His

fellow marshal and foster brother was seated in the corner of the desk-clogged room. Harlan's attention was on some reports, but judging from his concerned look, he'd given Clayton a glance or two.

That's when Clayton realized he'd slipped his hand over the Glock in his leather waist holster.

Old habits.

Sometimes he wished he could turn off this blasted LEO—law enforcement officer—alarm in his head, but he'd been a marshal for nearly a decade now. Too long to turn off alarms. Or to get a decent night's sleep, for that matter.

"I'm not sure if everything's okay," Clayton answered. "I got a bad feeling about this."

And that sent Harlan from his desk and to the window, where he looked out, as well.

Clayton waited, watching the wipers on the truck slash away the rain from the windshield. Not a gentle April shower. More like a downpour. But it wasn't long before he heard the footsteps on the stairs. Not just ordinary footsteps, though.

Heels.

They really stood out in the building where all six of the marshals were male. There were female employees in the other parts of the building, but this time of day they rarely came to the second floor.

The woman stepped into the doorway of the squad room, her attention zooming right to Clayton.

Lenora.

Yeah, it was her, all right. She stood there, her damp shoulder-length brown hair clinging to the sides of her face. The water dripped from her raincoat and the umbrella she had clutched in her hand and splattered onto the floor.

"Clayton," she said on a rise of breath.

Her gaze darted to Harlan, and she cleared her throat. Maybe because Harlan was just plain intimidating, with his linebacker-size body and hard lawman's eyes. Thankfully, Clayton's foster brother went back to his desk in the corner and pretended not to notice they were in the room.

"Marshal Caldwell," Lenora corrected herself.

That surprised him. Women he'd had sex with didn't usually get so formal after the fact. Of course, Lenora and he had only been together for that one night—and at one of the worst times in her life, to boot—but still she had to remember it.

He certainly did.

Despite being all mussed and wet, Lenora was a darn attractive woman. And judging from her dark green eyes, a troubled one.

"There've been no updates on the investigation," Clayton volunteered to test her reaction. Was that why she'd asked to see him?

Clayton glanced at Harlan, who was glancing at them and no doubt wondering what the heck was going on.

So was Clayton.

Lenora had been cryptic when she'd called the day before, saying only that she needed to *catch up* with him.

"No updates," she repeated. "Yes." And that was all she said for several seconds, before she cleared her throat again. "Marshal Walker called a few weeks ago to say there'd been no progress."

Marshal Walker, as in Dallas Walker, another of Clayton's foster brothers. Dallas was indeed in charge of the investigation into the murder of Lenora's best friend. A murder that'd happened nearly two months ago.

The last time Clayton had seen Lenora.

And they hadn't exactly parted under good circumstances. In fact, Lenora had sneaked out of the hotel room while Clayton was in the shower, and she'd left him a note saying it'd been a big mistake for them to have sex.

Since that wasn't exactly a good memory, Clayton pushed it aside and hitched his thumb toward the window. "Did someone in a black pickup follow you here?"

Lenora's eyes widened, and she practically ran across the room to look out.

No truck.

"Sorry," he mumbled. "It was there a few seconds ago. Guess I was wrong about it." Funny, though, his LEO alarm was usually a hundred percent.

Lenora was breathing through her mouth now, and her eyes were still wide. Her gaze darted around the parking lot and street. "You thought I was being followed?"

"Were you?"

"Maybe." Her bottom lip trembled. "I'd hoped it was my imagination. I'm not sleeping well, and the nightmares are getting worse."

Yeah. He knew all about those nightmares. A woman, Jill Lang, was dead. Gunned down right in front of both of them. She'd been Lenora's best friend. And a witness in Clayton's protective custody.

He didn't expect the nightmares to end anytime soon.

Clayton could practically feel Lenora's worry, and even though she'd given him the brush-off two months ago, he reached out and touched her arm. Well, the sleeve of her wet raincoat, anyway. He hoped it was a sympathetic gesture without getting too close.

"Jill's killer was caught," Clayton reminded her. And

even though the man had yet to go to trial, he would be convicted of murder. No doubt about that, since there was a mountain of evidence against him, including Clayton's and Lenora's own eyewitness accounts.

But maybe this wasn't about Jill's killer.

"I know about the break-ins at your house in Eagle Pass," Clayton told her.

Lenora pulled her shoulders back, and she shook her head. "How? Why?"

Both good questions. He didn't exactly have good answers, though, and it sounded a little creepy to admit that he'd kept tabs on her. But he had. Too bad Clayton didn't know exactly why he'd done it. He'd had short-term relationships before that he'd dismissed without a second thought.

So why hadn't he been able to do that with Lenora?

Because there was something that wasn't quite right about this. Something he couldn't put his finger on.

She pushed her hair from her face and glanced at Harlan again. "Could we go somewhere private and talk?" she asked Clayton.

Maybe Harlan was making her nervous. He had that effect on people. But from Clayton's assessment, Lenora had been nervous before she even came into the room.

Clayton set his coffee on his desk and grabbed his jacket. "There's a diner across the street," he said, already walking toward the door. "Call me if something comes up," he added to Harlan.

"Tell me about these break-ins," Clayton insisted as soon as they were out of the office.

Lenora gave a weary sigh. "The first one happened last week—as I'm sure you read in the report. I wasn't there, but the person destroyed an antique panel that I'd been restoring."

Property damage. Much better than damaging her body, but he could tell from her tone that it still hurt. Clayton didn't know a lot about Lenora's job in stained-glass restoration, but he remembered her saying that she often worked with expensive antiques.

"What about the second break-in?" He stopped just outside the building and looked around. Lenora did, too. There was no sign of that black truck, so he took her by arm and led her across the street.

"You already know." She sounded upset, or something, that he'd read the police reports, but Clayton didn't intend to apologize for that.

"I still consider you my business," he clarified.

She blinked. "Why? Because my friend was killed on your watch? If so, that wasn't your fault."

The question threw him. Yeah, that was part of it—that a woman in his protective custody had died. In fact, that should have been *all* of it. But there were feelings buried beneath this, and maybe Lenora's blink meant it wasn't all business for her, either.

She looked away, mumbled something he didn't catch. "Back to the break-ins. Again, I wasn't there for the second one. In fact, I've been living at one of those extended-stay hotels since the first break-in." Lenora paused. "The intruder left threatening messages scrawled on my bedroom wall."

Clayton cursed. That hadn't been in the initial report he'd read from the Eagle Pass P.D., but Clayton knew this was an escalation. If Lenora had been there—

But he cut off that bad thought.

Maybe their one-night stand had made her want to keep some distance between them. But she was here now, and though she hadn't said it specifically, she appeared to be asking for his help.

Which she would get.

And Clayton assured himself that it had nothing to do with the night he'd spent with her. Or this cool heat still simmering between them. He would have helped anyone who needed it.

They took a booth by the window so he could keep watch for the truck, and he asked the waitress to bring them two cups of coffee.

"Do the cops have a suspect in the break-ins?" he asked.

Lenora shook her head. "They don't have any prints, any type of trace evidence, and none of my neighbors saw anyone suspicious."

That meshed with the reports he'd read, but witnesses often came forward later. Maybe that would happen in this case.

"Tell me who you think was in that truck," Clayton said.

Another head shake. "I don't know."

"A boyfriend, maybe?"

"No. I'm not seeing anyone. And I don't think I've been followed before." Lenora blew out another breath, and she had a death grip on the coffee cup. "There's more." She said it so softly that Clayton didn't actually hear her. He saw the words form on her lips.

"What?" he pushed when she didn't explain.

This was beyond a bad feeling, and he instantly went back to the night they'd spent together. He wasn't sure he was ready to deal with what she was about to say, but he also knew he had to hear it.

"You're pregnant?" he came out and asked.

No blink this time. She nodded.

And that nod sent his heartbeat racing out of control. *Oh, man.*

It felt as if someone had punched him in the gut. All the air left his lungs. *All*. But he fought to get enough breath so he could speak.

However, Lenora beat him to it. "I wrestled with whether to tell you at all. I mean, we hardly know each other. But I decided if our situations were reversed, I'd want to know. By the way, I don't expect anything from you," she added.

That gave him a jolt of breath he needed. "Well, you damn well should expect something."

Lenora eased back, her attention fixed to him. "Obviously, you're not pleased about this—"

"Only because I didn't see it coming."

"Yes." And she repeated that. "It caught me off guard, too. We used protection, but something must have gone wrong."

Obviously.

He pulled in a couple of quick breaths and hoped it'd clear his head. He needed to think. To say the right thing.

Whatever that was.

A baby!

He'd never planned on being a father. Never. And this was a shock that made him speechless.

She looked up. Their gazes connected. But then Lenora looked away again. Not at the coffee this time, but rather out the window.

"Is that the black truck you saw?" Her attention was on something over his shoulder.

Clayton turned in that direction and saw the truck. Yeah. It was the same one. It was creeping along Main Street, going past the diner.

Unlike before, the window on the passenger's side was halfway down. There didn't appear to be anyone seated there, only the person behind the steering wheel. Clayton couldn't see the guy's face.

But he saw the gun.

"Get down!" Clayton shouted to Lenora and everyone else in the diner.

He reached beneath his jacket to draw his Glock, but it was already too late. The bullet blasted through the window.

Clayton felt the sharp pain in the side of his head, and even over the blast, he heard Lenora yell. He tried to move. Tried to return fire and protect her, but he felt himself falling.

And everything around him turned cold and gray.

Chapter Two

Lenora's heart slammed against her chest, and she snatched up the Glock that dropped from Clayton's hand and onto the table. She saw the blood, no way to miss that.

No way to avoid that punch of adrenaline, either.

That fear.

Oh, God.

Clayton had been shot.

That was her first thought, quickly followed by the realization that this could all be her fault. But she shoved those things aside because every second counted now.

"Call an ambulance!" Lenora yelled out to no one in particular.

She couldn't let this guy get off another shot. She had to stop him, or he could kill Clayton, her and anyone who was unlucky enough to be near them.

Lenora took aim at the truck.

And she fired.

The shot blistered through the air, but it was practically drowned out by the screams and shouts from the other diners. Lenora couldn't be sure, but she thought she managed to shoot the guy in the arm. She took aim again, but the driver hit the accelerator, and with the tires squealing against the wet asphalt, he fishtailed away.

She scrambled across the table, catching Clayton as he slumped to the side. There was even more blood now. And it wasn't in a good place, either.

He'd been shot in the head.

No. This couldn't be happening.

With her heartbeat pounding in her ears and her hands shaking, Lenora kept watch to make sure the shooter didn't return for a second round. She couldn't risk that.

She jerked the scarf from around her neck and lightly pressed it to Clayton's wound. She couldn't add too much pressure, because it might embed the bullet even deeper. It might even kill him.

If he wasn't dead already.

"Clayton?" She choked back a sob and tilted back his head a little. No response, so she pressed her fingers to his neck.

He was alive.

Thank God.

But he needed a doctor immediately.

"Get that ambulance here," she shouted, though she figured it was already on the way. Still, it couldn't arrive soon enough, because every second counted now.

A dozen thoughts went through her mind. None of them good. It had only been two months since her friend Jill had been gunned down just like this. Right in front of her. In front of Clayton, too. This had to have a different ending than that shooting.

Somehow, someway, Clayton had to survive this.

"Clayton?" she repeated. "Can you hear me?"

He turned his head toward her, and his lips moved, too. He mumbled something that Lenora couldn't understand, so she put her ear closer to his mouth.

"I'm so sorry," she whispered.

That seemed to get his attention, and he tried to open his eyes. "The baby." The two words didn't have any sound, but she was pretty sure that's what he was trying to say.

The baby.

The reason for this visit. Lenora had dreaded coming here. Telling him. And had braced herself for his reaction. But now she had a different reason to dread why she'd decided to tell him.

If she hadn't come here, this might not have happened.

From the corner of her eye, she saw the movement of the man approaching and nearly lifted the gun again before she realized it was Marshal Harlan McKinney. With his own gun drawn and holding his cell to his ear, he raced across the street toward the diner and had to dodge a car that nearly plowed right into him.

"Get here now!" Harlan shouted into his phone.

"The driver of that black truck," Lenora managed to say. "He shot Clayton."

"I saw it from the window," Harlan mumbled, and he practically pushed her aside so he could take hold of his foster brother. The fear was right there, in his eyes and in every part of his body.

"Hold on, Clayton," Harlan said. "The ambulance should be here any minute." His gaze flashed to her. "Why'd this happen?"

"I'm not sure."

"Then guess!" Harlan insisted. "Because I want to know why my brother was shot."

But Lenora didn't even get a chance to speculate.

Or lie.

She heard a welcome sound. The ambulance sirens wailed from up the street, and it didn't take long for the vehicle to screech to a stop directly in front of the diner. Two medics got out and came rushing toward them.

Harlan and she stepped back out of the way, and Lenora watched. Prayed. And tried to keep it together. In addition to the flashbacks and the fear crawling through her, she thought she might throw up.

Bad timing.

She'd had few symptoms of the pregnancy, and she didn't want to be queasy now when so much was at stake.

"Marshal Caldwell?" one of the medics said to Clayton.

Still no response.

"Clayton?" Harlan tried.

And this time Lenora saw his eyelids flutter and open just slightly. Clayton's coffee-colored eyes were unfocused, glazed, but he turned them in his brother's direction.

"You'll be okay," Harlan assured him.

Lenora prayed that was true.

Clayton mumbled something. Or rather he tried, but like before Lenora couldn't hear what he said. The medics moved in front of her, easing Clayton onto the gurney, and they hurried to the ambulance with him.

Lenora moved, too. She didn't want to lose sight of him, and apparently neither did Harlan, because he latched on to her arm and dragged her into the back of the ambulance with him. He didn't ask them for permission to ride.

The ambulance sped away from the diner, and Harlan and she watched as the medics took Clayton's vitals.

"You returned fire," Harlan said and held out his hand. "I'll need Clayton's gun."

For a moment Lenora had forgotten that she was still

clutching it. She had to force her hand to open, and she gave the Glock to him.

"Not a smart thing to do," Harlan snarled. "Discharging a firearm in a crowd."

"There weren't any bystanders in my line of sight," she blurted out, wishing that she hadn't, because it brought Harlan's attention directly to her.

"Why did you come to see Clayton?" he demanded.

The truth would only lead to more questions, and she didn't want to be interrogated by this particular marshal. "Two months ago, my friend was murdered. I wanted to know if there'd been any new developments. I wanted to make sure her killer would stay in jail."

Harlan no doubt knew all about Jill and the investigation. He stared at her, suspicion in his eyes, and Lenora had enough instincts to know that if Harlan's foster brother hadn't been just a few feet away and bleeding from a head wound, he would have called her a liar.

She was.

And Harlan would have pushed for a better answer than the one she'd just told him.

But there was no reason for her to tell this man about the pregnancy. When Clayton was better, he could break the news to his family. And he could also decide if he wanted to be part of this baby's life.

If Clayton survived, that was.

She stared at the father of her unborn child. The man she'd slept with because she'd been too distraught to make a logical decision.

Sex wasn't always logical, though.

Neither was the attraction she'd felt for this lawman. The attraction had been instant. Probably because he had rock-star looks to go along with that cowboy attitude. Or maybe it was because she'd felt this, well, connection with him. Connection aside, it'd been beyond stupid to sleep with him. She should have just walked away. Should have written Clayton and this attraction right out of her life.

That would have been the safe thing to do.

But she hadn't. And now he was lying on a gurney, maybe dying.

Harlan's phone buzzed, and while he took the call, Lenora moved slightly closer so she could get a better look at Clayton. There was blood on his dark brown hair, on the side of his face as well, but the flow was barely a trickle now. She had no idea if that was good or bad. The only experience she had with head wounds was they were usually fatal.

"That was Dallas," Harlan said when he finished the call. "Marshal Walker," he added, but Lenora already knew who Harlan meant. Another of Clayton's foster brothers. Another federal marshal.

In fact, Clayton had five foster brothers, all of whom were U.S. marshals. That would mean five sets of questions, and each of them would deserve answers as to why one of their own had been shot while having a cup of coffee with her.

"They found the shooter," Harlan added. "He wrecked his truck only about four blocks from the diner."

Lenora certainly hadn't expected that and would have thought the guy would manage to get out of the area. "Who is he?"

"According to the ID in his wallet, his name is Corey Dayton. Ring any bells?"

"No." And that wasn't a lie. Of course, the ID could be fake, and she might recognize his real name. "Does your brother have him in custody?"

Harlan shook his head. "He's dead."

Lenora pulled in her breath. "From the bullet I put in him?"

"Maybe. But he wasn't wearing a seat belt, and he crashed into a parked garbage truck."

Part of her was relieved that the man who'd shot Clayton was out of the picture, but a dead man couldn't give them answers, and Lenora very much wanted to know why this guy had fired into the diner.

"Tell me," Harlan said, "is this connected to your friend's murder?"

"I'm not sure," she answered honestly. "When you can, you'll want to question the man who murdered Jill. Adam Riggs," she supplied, though Harlan no doubt knew the name of the man behind bars. And he would absolutely question him.

When his brother was out of the woods.

It was possible that Riggs had hired the shooter, maybe because Riggs was riled that Clayton had arrested him for Jill's murder. If so, Harlan and the other marshals would soon find that connection.

So would Lenora.

She'd find it, and if Riggs was responsible, then he was going to pay, and pay hard.

Of course, Riggs could have hired someone to aim that shot at her, too, because he might believe that as Jill's friend she'd helped catch him. She hadn't. But there was a lot of twisted stuff in a killer's mind. Especially this killer's.

"Are there any loose ends with Jill's murder?" Harlan asked.

Lenora knew where this was leading—the marshal was looking for quick answers. But she didn't have them.

"Maybe I'm the loose end." Lenora had to pause, take

a breath and choose her words carefully. "Jill worked for Adam Riggs and discovered he was into big-time money laundering. She was about to testify against him when he shot and killed her."

Lenora saw those images as clearly as she saw Clayton in front of her. God, when was this going to end?

"Clayton put you in protective custody along with Jill," Harlan supplied. "Because he thought Riggs might use you to get Jill to back off her testimony."

"He would have," Lenora confirmed. "But killing Clayton and me now accomplishes nothing." At least nothing that she was aware of.

Still, something wasn't right about this.

But what?

What was she missing?

Maybe it didn't even matter. What mattered was that Clayton had been safe until she'd arrived to tell him about the baby.

She saw Clayton's hand move, and Lenora leaned in. Clayton's eyes were open now. Still a little dazed looking. But he looked directly at his brother, who'd moved to her side.

"What happened?" Clayton asked Harlan.

It such a simple question, but it caused relief to flood through Lenora. Clayton wasn't just conscious, he was talking.

"You were shot," Harlan answered. The words didn't come easily. His voice was clogged with emotion. "We'll be at the hospital soon. You'll be okay."

Clayton stayed quiet a few seconds, shook his head and then tried to get off the gurney. The medics quickly stopped him from doing that.

"I have to go," Clayton insisted. Definitely no slurred

words now. He seemed like the determined, focused lawman that she knew. "I have a witness to protect."

Well, focused except for that last part. Maybe he didn't realize he'd been shot.

"Jill Lang," Clayton added and tried to get up again. "I have to protect her."

Lenora froze. Why would Clayton mention Jill's name? Obviously he wasn't as coherent as she'd thought, because Jill had been dead for two months.

"I have to protect her friend, too," Clayton insisted while the medics held him down. "I have to protect Lenora Whitaker."

Clayton certainly didn't say her name as he had earlier. It sounded foreign on his lips.

As if he'd spoken the name of a stranger.

"Lenora's here," Harlan said, inching her closer so that Clayton could see her face. "She's okay. She wasn't hurt in the shooting."

Clayton stared at her, and even though his eyes were indeed clear, something was missing. He shook his head, his stare aimed right at her.

"You," Clayton said. He winced, took a deep breath.

"Yes," Lenora answered. "It's me."

But he only shook his head again. "Who are you?" Clayton asked.

Lenora froze.

Oh, mercy. He hadn't just said her name as if they'd never met—the look he was giving her certainly wasn't a familiar one, either.

It was like looking into the eyes of a stranger.

"Who are you?" Clayton repeated with his attention fastened to Lenora. "And why are you here?"

Chapter Three

Three Months Later

Clayton spotted the woman on the stepladder perched in front of the stained-glass window inside the country church. She was about five-six. Dark brown hair. Average build. Well, average build from what he could tell. She wore a drab green lab-style coat over her jeans.

He stayed back behind the last row of pews so that she wouldn't see him, but he could see her.

The light in the church was dim, thank goodness, so Clayton was able to remove his sunglasses, but he was careful to dodge the lines of sunlight piercing through the beveled glass around the window panels. The last thing he needed was a migraine. Even the mild ones were a bear, and something he'd had to deal with since the shooting. Today he didn't want to deal with the pain.

He wanted to deal with this woman who might have answers.

Clayton waited, watched until she finally put her soldering iron aside and pulled off the mask that'd covered her nose and mouth.

It was Lenora Whitaker, all right.

Keeping a firm grip on the sides of the ladder, she stepped down to the floor, propped her hands on her hips and looked up at the glass angel's wing that she'd just repaired. She must have been pleased with the results, because she nodded, smiled. Turned.

The color drained from her face. The smile, too. Almost as if she'd seen a ghost.

"Clayton," she said in a rough whisper.

Well, at least she remembered him. Clayton wished he could say the same about her. Yeah, he knew those features because of the surveillance footage he'd studied, but he didn't recognize her.

Still, there was something familiar about her that went beyond recorded images. Maybe because she'd once been in his protective custody.

Something else he couldn't remember.

She didn't come closer, but pulled a rag from her coat pocket and wiped her hands. She also dodged his gaze. "How are you?"

"Better than the last time you saw me."

That brought her gaze back to his. "You got your memory back?"

He lifted his shoulder. "Some of it." Including all of his childhood, even the rotten parts. Most of adulthood, too. "Not about you, though."

Clayton paused, studied her expression. Her forehead was bunched up, and while there was concern in her eyes, there was also discomfort.

Probably because he'd found her.

"According to Harlan's account," Clayton said, "you didn't hang around long after I was shot."

She nodded, swallowed hard. "But I called, to find out that you'd made it out of surgery."

Yeah. Harlan had told him that, too. But what was missing were the details.

"How'd you find me?" She turned away from him

and started to gather her supplies, which she stuffed into a metal toolbox.

"It wasn't easy." In fact, it'd been downright hard. Clayton tipped his head to the stained-glass panel. "Not many people do the kind of work you do, so I kept calling churches and other places that have this sort of thing."

And he'd finally located her through a supplier who was billing a minister in the small town of Sadler's Falls for repairs to an antique stained-glass window. Lenora's area of expertise.

"I called the minister," Clayton explained. "And I posed as someone interested in a getting a referral for some stained-glass repairs needed on a house I'm restoring. He told me about this woman he'd just hired, but I didn't know it was you until I saw you just now." He paused. "You're using a fake name."

"Yes. After what happened, I thought it was the safe thing to do."

Probably. But Clayton still needed answers that he hadn't been able to get from anyone else.

She glanced at the scar on his forehead. It had faded considerably since his surgery three months earlier, but it was a reminder of just how close he'd come to dying.

"I've been looking for updates about the shooting," she said, "but the marshals still haven't found the person that hired the gunman who put a bullet in you."

"That's true." Not from lack of trying, though. The investigation had been a priority for his foster brothers. And now for Clayton. "But I thought you'd be able to help with that."

Lenora quickly shook her head. "I can't. I have no idea who's behind this."

"I'm not sure I believe that."

The pulse in her throat jumped, but before she could repeat her denial, Clayton walked closer, his cowboy boots thudding on the scarred hardwood floors of the old church.

Lenora backed up, and she pulled the sides of the coat closer, hugging it against her body. "You're accusing me of lying."

"Yeah," he readily admitted, and he held out his phone so she could see the video that he'd loaded. "The diner where I was shot doesn't have a security camera, but there were plenty of them on the Marshals building across the street."

And thanks to one of those cameras, he could show her the footage of them sitting down in the booth directly in front of the window.

"I understand we sat in that particular spot so I could watch for the black truck that I thought had been following you," he explained.

She nodded but didn't say anything. Lenora just watched. There was no audio, but it was clear that Lenora and he were talking in the diner. Clayton waited until the feed got to the first stopping point, then paused the video. He zoomed into his expression.

"I don't need a body-language expert to tell me that I'm surprised there. Shocked, actually." He dipped his head down slightly, forcing eye contact. "What did you say to me to put that look on my face?"

She didn't glance away this time. He was watching her closely. It seemed as if she was having a serious debate with herself—a debate that didn't turn out well for Clayton, because he saw the exact moment when she decided to lie.

"I can't remember specifically what I said, but we

were talking about the break-ins at the place where I used to live."

He didn't doubt that had come up in conversation—Clayton had read the reports of both break-ins—but since he'd already known about them before Lenora showed up at his office that morning, there probably wasn't much she could have told him that would have shocked him.

So why was she lying?

This was one area where Harlan hadn't been able to help. His brother had been in the office the morning of the visit, but he hadn't been privy to what Lenora and he had discussed. Too bad. Because Clayton had the feeling that it was more than important, and he wasn't letting her out of his sight until he had answers.

Clayton hit Play on the video, and they watched in silence. Well, verbal silence anyway. Lenora was glancing at him from the corner of her eye. He was doing the same, trying to remember anything and everything about her. She certainly didn't feel like a stranger. And her scent…

That was familiar, too.

Maybe it was his imagination, but that scent seemed to trigger other things. Like the memory of her taste. But that couldn't have happened. According to every report he'd read, the first time he met Lenora and her friend Jill was when they'd been placed in his protective custody. He wouldn't have kissed a woman on the job.

Maybe afterward.

After Jill had been murdered. After her shooter had been arrested and put behind bars. Yeah, he could maybe see it happening then, if Lenora had landed in his arms so he could comfort her.

But had they done that?

And if so, why hadn't Lenora admitted it?

He heard the slight shiver of her breath and looked down at the screen. Their recorded conversation was over, and both had noticed the approaching black truck. Though it was damn hard to watch, Clayton did. And he saw the impact of the bullet as it slammed into his head.

Lenora turned away, or rather started to do that, but Clayton caught her arm, keeping her in place. "Watch," he insisted.

She did, but from the corner of her eye, and it seemed as if she was genuinely horrified by what she was seeing. Him, slumped against the table, and her, grabbing his gun to return fire.

Clayton hit Pause again the second she pulled the trigger.

It was a clear image of not just the truck but of Lenora. The way she was holding the gun. The expression on her face. The precision with which she returned fire.

"There are only two types of people who react that way in a life-or-death situation," he said. "Law enforcement and criminals."

She didn't ask which he thought she was and didn't deny his conclusion. Lenora mumbled something, shook her head and walked away from him.

"I need some air," she said. Before he could stop her, she went to the side door just a few feet away and threw it open.

The hot July sunlight speared through the tiny church.

Clayton couldn't quite choke back a groan, and he shoved on his glasses. Too late, though. The pain came.

"What's wrong?" Lenora immediately asked.

He turned away, fought back the throbbing in his head. Maybe it wouldn't turn into a full-blown migraine.

"The sunlight," he managed to say. "I get headaches."

She jerked the door closed and hurried back to him. "From the gunshot?"

He nodded and forced out some hard breaths. Sometimes it helped.

"I'm sorry," she whispered. "I didn't know. That wasn't in any of the reports I read about you."

Even through the blinding pain that got his attention, and he stared at her.

"Yes, I read reports about you," she verified. "I wanted to make sure you were okay."

"You could have just asked. Or stayed at the hospital until I came out of surgery. Instead, Harlan said you bolted from the ambulance the second it stopped."

"I did." She looked away, repeated it. Lenora turned again, as if looking for a way out, and the movement caused her coat to shift to the side.

Despite the pain, Clayton pulled off his glasses so he could make sure his eyes weren't playing tricks on him. They weren't. He saw her belly.

Or rather, the baby bump.

It wasn't huge, but it was there. And even more, Lenora followed his stunned gaze and pulled the coat back over her. The little gasping sound she made didn't help steady his nerves, either.

"You're pregnant," Clayton said.

She nodded.

"How far along are you?" he asked when she didn't volunteer anything else.

Lenora didn't jump to answer that, either. "Second trimester."

He stared at her. "That's what—four or five months?"

Another hesitation. "Nearly five."

The brain injury might have robbed him of some of

his memories, but he could still do basic math. Nearly five months ago put it just about the time she'd been in his protective custody.

The time frame that was a blank spot in his mind.

"How much do you remember about me?" she asked before he could say anything.

"Not much. Nothing," he amended. "Everything I know about you I learned from the reports and surveillance videos. And from Adam Riggs."

Clearly, she hadn't been expecting that last part, because she sucked in a quick breath. "What did Riggs tell you about me?"

Not as much as Clayton had wanted. And while Clayton would answer her questions about Riggs, he wasn't forgetting about that baby bump. He would get answers about that before this conversation was over.

"I went to visit Riggs in jail," Clayton explained, "to try to figure out if he was responsible for shooting me. Of course, he said he wasn't."

"Of course." She huffed. "Anything that comes out of his mouth is a lie, because he's a cold-blooded killer."

Clayton couldn't argue with that. He didn't remember Riggs gunning down Jill Lang, but he'd seen the crime-scene photos and read the reports. The man was indeed a murderer.

One behind bars.

And one that shouldn't have had the access to hire a gun to come after Lenora and him.

"Riggs said you 'had secrets,' and that's a direct quote," Clayton finished. "Any idea what he meant by that?"

He purposely dropped his gaze to her stomach. He doubted that bump had anything to do with Riggs's cryptic comment, but Clayton figured Lenora definitely had some secrets that needed to be spilled.

She opened her mouth, closed it and then groaned. "I did you a favor by leaving Maverick Springs. My advice—let me keep doing you that favor."

Clayton stepped in front of her when she tried to leave. Yeah, he could restrain her, but if she opened a door, the sunlight was going to cause the pain to spike again and maybe send him to his knees. After that, he wouldn't be able to do much of anything. Ironic that a bullet hadn't stopped him, but now sunlight could.

"Did we have sex?" he came right out and asked. "And is that my baby you're carrying?"

The questions came easily enough, but there was nothing easy about the emotions whipping through him. He'd come here for answers about the attack and why she'd disappeared, but Clayton hadn't been prepared for this.

Except there was something familiar about this, too.

A sense of déjà vu, and since he'd never fathered a child, he had to think that maybe the reason Lenora had visited him three months ago was to tell him she was pregnant. That would certainly explain the stunned look on his face in the surveillance video.

"You don't have to do this," Lenora said, her voice like a plea. "Just go home and heal. I don't want you to get hurt again."

Well, the woman knew how to keep him on his toes. He really wanted to know what she meant by that last remark, but first things first.

"Is that my baby?" he demanded.

Her mouth tightened. "We had a one-night stand after Jill was murdered."

The emotions whipped harder through him. "I'll take

that as a yes." He cursed, and it was more than several moments before he could regain enough control to speak.

"You should have told me—again," he added. "After I came out of surgery."

"You had enough to deal with."

That answer didn't help. "What were you going to do? Have the baby and not let me know?"

"I would have told you eventually. When you were better."

He leaned in and yanked off his glasses so he could meet her eye to eye. "I'm better, and I've been better for a while now."

She nodded, but there was no agreement in any part of her body language. "Knowing the truth doesn't make this situation *better* or easier. But it does make it more dangerous."

Clayton made a circling motion with his fingers for her to continue.

She did, eventually. "I can't prove it, but Riggs might have hired the shooter to kill me, and he might have shot you by mistake. And if that's true, then it's not safe for you to be around me."

"That's a big *maybe*. Riggs has just as much reason to want me dead as he does you. After all, we both saw him gun down Jill. We'll both testify against him."

"You remember the shooting?" she asked.

Unfortunately. "Yes." However, there were gaps both before and after the murder. Big gaps that Riggs probably didn't know he had. Hopefully, his lawyers wouldn't, either, because Clayton didn't want his testimony called into question.

She groaned softly. "But why didn't Riggs come after

you before that day at the diner? Why did he wait until we were together?"

"I don't know. But that's something we could have worked out if you'd stayed—"

"No, it's not," Lenora interrupted. She waited until his gaze came back to hers. "Riggs was right. I do have secrets. I'm not who you think I am."

Oh, man. He didn't like that tone or the look in her eyes. "What do you mean?"

"It's all lies. Not the baby. That's the only truth in all of this." She tipped her head to his phone, where the video of her returning fire was frozen on the screen. "You said only a criminal or someone in law enforcement would have reacted that way."

Clayton nodded. Waited. "And which one are you?"

Lenora's bottom lip trembled. "Both."

Chapter Four

"Both?" Clayton repeated.

Lenora saw the instant concern in his eyes. Not ordinary concern, either. The kind of concern a marshal would have when facing down someone on the other side of the law.

"Explain that," he demanded. His gaze dropped to her stomach. "And then we'll discuss the baby."

Lenora didn't know which part of the intended discussion she dreaded most, but her dread was a drop in the bucket compared to her fear that Clayton's mere presence here could get him killed.

"Are you sure no one followed you?" Lenora didn't wait for his answer. She went to the sliver of a side window by the front door and peered out. The beveled glass distorted the view, but she saw her own car. No one else's, and definitely no sign of a gunman. But that didn't mean there wasn't one.

"I parked on the other side of the cemetery," Clayton explained. "I didn't see anyone following me, and I was careful." He paused. "But there's always the possibility that someone used the same steps I did to find you."

True. That didn't do much to steady her already racing heart and frazzled nerves. Lenora made a mental note to call the minister, Reverend Donaldson, to say she couldn't finish the job. Then she could leave town and make sure Clayton didn't find her again. However, that leaving part wasn't going to happen unless she gave him the answers he was demanding, because there was no way he'd just let her walk out.

But where to start?

It was a tangled mess. One that Clayton definitely wasn't going to like.

She took a deep breath, walked back toward him and sank down into a pew. "Jill and I both worked for the justice department." There. Plain and simple. She gave him a moment to let that sink in.

It obviously didn't sink in well. Clayton's eyes narrowed. "It's the first I'm hearing of this, and that's funny since I work for the justice department, too, and I was assigned to protect you two."

Yes, she was painfully aware of that. "You weren't told the whole truth, and I was sworn to secrecy. Jill and I were agents on a special task force put together to bring down Adam Riggs and his cronies—"

"Any reason I wasn't let in on this?"

"A good one." Well, it was good in some people's minds. It'd never felt right to her. "There were other agents planted in companies that Riggs was doing business with. The task-force supervisor didn't want anyone knowing that Jill and I were deep cover, because it might have leaked—"

"I wouldn't have leaked it," he snapped, interrupting her again. He slipped his sunglasses back on and went to the front windows to look out.

The sunglasses were an odd mix with the rest of his clothes: the jeans, boots and silver rodeo belt. He used the brim of his black Stetson to help shield his eyes. It made her wonder just how bad his headaches actually were and if he was duty ready. Apparently he'd been ready enough to find her, and she'd thought she had covered her tracks well with the assumed name and the cash-only lifestyle.

"You could have trusted me," Clayton added.

"I know that *now,* but we didn't know it at the time. The task-force supervisor also wanted to make it look as if Jill and I were truly just workers who might be in danger because of a federal investigation. That's why he asked the Marshals Service to provide protection for us. He took the 'better safe than sorry' approach."

Clayton shook his head, glanced back at her, and even though she couldn't actually see his eyes behind those shades, she was certain he was glaring. "That didn't work out so well, did it?"

No, it hadn't. Somehow Lenora would have to learn to live with that, but she hadn't had much luck doing it so far. The nightmares were still there. Every night. Unrelenting.

"So, you're an agent," Clayton said almost like a challenge.

"*Former* agent. I resigned shortly after Jill was murdered. But before the justice department, I worked in Dallas for a man who was a world-class money launderer. And I helped him."

Lenora nearly choked on the confession, but it was true. She had indeed helped him, unknowingly, but she darn well should have known what he was up to. She'd played with fire and had gotten burned.

Now Lenora was trying to make sure that didn't happen again.

Yes, Clayton was fire, all right.

Fiery trouble in a black Stetson.

All of her experience and training told her that he

was off-limits. As if on cue, the baby kicked, reminding her that the hands-off rule had been broken months ago. Still, that didn't mean she couldn't do something to stop more bad things from happening. She didn't include her baby in that "bad things" department. She desperately loved and wanted this child. But the baby's father was a different matter entirely.

She couldn't live with another death on her hands. Especially his death.

"And you were a criminal?" he mumbled. He shook his head, put his back to the sidelight window and shucked off his glasses so his gaze could meet hers.

Yes, it was a glare, all right.

Lenora nodded. "When the feds started investigating the money-laundering scheme I was involved in, I was taken into custody and cut a deal to help them with an investigation to collar my boss."

"Sounds dangerous," he pointed out.

She settled for a shrug. "My boss and his business partners were bigger fish that they wanted. So, because the situation could have turned, well, more than dangerous, they trained me like a regular agent. But I was technically just a criminal informant assigned to the deep-cover task force. Then, after my boss was arrested and convicted, they asked me to stay on in the department and work on the Riggs case."

Clayton made a sound of displeasure. "And as a dupe, my own people assigned me to two women that I was told needed protection."

"Obviously, we did need it, because one of us was murdered," she reminded him, then paused. "I'm sorry I had to lie to you."

"Not as sorry as I am. I hate being lied to, especially by people that I'm supposed to trust." However, he immediately added a sound of dismissal. "Old baggage rearing its head. But it still comes into play here."

She knew a little about his old childhood baggage, from the notorious Rocky Creek Children's Facility, which was now closed. Had been for sixteen years. She also knew his mother had died giving birth to him and that his father, Melvin Larson, had literally abandoned him at the facility when he was eleven. All of that had come out when they'd talked in bed after their fast and furious bout of sex.

Too bad her memories of that were crystal clear.

She could remember every last detail of that night. The raw pain from losing a friend and fellow agent. The comfort she'd found in Clayton's arms. The pleasure, too. Pleasure should have been the last thing on her mind that night, but she'd felt plenty of it anyway. Thanks to Clayton.

"Lies like that are usually unnecessary," he tossed out to her.

"You lied to the minister to find me," Lenora tossed right back at him.

He gave her that riled look again, like the one he'd given her in the diner. "I didn't lie to deceive. I lied to find you so I could help. Maybe now's a good time to ask if you were planning on telling me any of this?"

No, it wasn't a good time to ask, but Lenora would answer it anyway. "I was waiting for you to heal and for the danger to die down."

He lifted his shoulder. "How the hell was the danger going to die down? You know who was responsible for putting that bullet in my head?"

She couldn't deny it fast enough. "No. I assumed that Riggs hired someone to do it, but I don't have any proof." Lenora stopped, met his gaze. "Do you?"

Clayton didn't answer her for several moments, but his stare continued to stab at her. At least it did until the baby kicked her and she winced a little. It wasn't a hard kick, but she'd only been feeling movement for a few weeks and wasn't used to it.

"You okay?" Clayton asked.

"Fine. The baby moved, that's all."

His mouth tightened. Then relaxed. He mumbled some profanity. "I'm having a hard time dealing with this."

"Of course." She didn't dare repeat the offer she'd made to him at the diner, that she expected nothing from him. No, best not to say it aloud, but the truth was, she *couldn't* expect anything from him. Because she needed him out of her life. Maybe just temporarily.

Maybe forever.

And that meant she needed to get on with her explanation. Besides, it was possible Clayton could actually help. She'd been hesitant to trust anyone, and maybe she was a fool for trusting him, but without this explanation, he clearly wasn't leaving.

"After your shooting, I wasn't sure whom I could trust." She slid her hand over her stomach.

Clayton huffed. "Any of my five foster brothers would have been a good start. They're all marshals and all capable of protecting you."

"But I didn't know them, and I wasn't sure I could trust anyone in law enforcement."

That eased Clayton's glare, and he cocked his eyebrow. "Why?"

"Because after you were shot, I tried to call my handler. My task-force leader," Lenora corrected. She'd always hated the term *handler*. It made her feel like a circus animal that needed to be controlled. "His name is James Britt, and he didn't return my call for two days."

Clayton stayed quiet a moment. "That's unusual?"

"Very, especially considering I left him a frantic message to call me immediately." She pushed her hair from her face. "But the truth is, I was concerned about James prior to that. He'd started to question me about what I really saw the night Jill was murdered. He seemed to try to make me doubt that Riggs was the one to pull the trigger."

"It was Riggs," Clayton verified. "I saw him, too."

Lenora nodded. "James knows that, but he kept pushing, as if he was looking for some kind of discrepancies in my report. I dismissed it, thinking he was just trying to prepare me for my testimony at the trial."

"That's possible," Clayton admitted.

Possible, yes, but Lenora hadn't been able to shake the bad feeling in the pit of her stomach.

"When James finally called me back after your shooting, he asked me if I'd gone back to *my old ways*. If I was running laundered money again. He wanted to know if I'd done something to get you shot. I didn't," she quickly added.

Clayton made a sound to indicate he was giving that some thought. "A few days before I was shot, someone broke into your place and vandalized it. I've been looking into any connection between that and the shooting, but I can't find it. Did you?"

She had to shake her head. "And I looked. The Eagle Pass police weren't able to get any prints or trace from the break-ins, so there was no arrest."

He continued to stare at her. "So your solution was to go into hiding."

"I had the baby to think about." And Lenora wasn't

going to apologize for that. "I didn't want to take any more risks than I'd already taken."

"And I wasn't around to help you." He blew out a long breath, stood and stared down at her. "Well, I'm around now, and I want you to go back to Maverick Springs with me, to my family's ranch."

Lenora got to her feet, too. "Didn't you hear what I said? It's too dangerous for me to come out of hiding and go with you. Obviously this person is after me, not you, because you've been out of the hospital for weeks now and no one has tried to kill you."

"Not yet. But I think we should get to the bottom of what's going on before we jump to conclusions. Maybe Riggs hasn't sent anyone else after me because he knows it wouldn't be a smart thing to do. After all, the last person who tried to kill me is dead. Thanks to you," he added.

Yeah. Thanks to her.

Too little, too late.

By the time she'd put a bullet in their attacker, Clayton had already been shot.

"I shouldn't have come there that day to tell you about the baby." Her voice cracked, and she cleared her throat. "But you're not the only one dealing with old baggage here. It played into my decision to tell you."

"Old baggage or not, you should have told me," he confirmed.

"But you don't even remember me, do you? You don't remember sleeping with me."

His gaze slid down her face to her body. Something different went through his eyes this time. Something she had no trouble recognizing.

Attraction.

Yes, she'd felt it, too, the first time she'd ever looked at him. And every time since.

She huffed, stood and would have gone to the window if it wouldn't have put them so close. "It hardly seemed fair to go waltzing into your hospital room to tell you that your one-night stand had led to an unexpected pregnancy. I wanted you to focus on your recovery."

"Maybe it wouldn't have been fair, but it would have been the right thing to do for the baby." The sunglasses went back on so he could have another look outside.

The right thing. In other words, turn over her safety— and the baby's—to him. Under normal circumstances she might have considered it, but it was crystal clear that Clayton was in no shape to be offering her protection.

Not yet anyway.

Her best bet was to regroup, go back into hiding under a different name. And a different job. One that couldn't be traced to anything in her past. Then, once things had settled down and his shooter was in custody, she could go to him and have him be part of their baby's life.

It seemed like a logical plan. But one look at Clayton's firm expression and she knew this would be a hard sell, if she could convince him at all. However, before she got a chance to sell anything, she saw Clayton shift his position. He leaned in closer to the glass.

"A dark blue SUV just parked at the end of the road," he relayed to her as he locked the front door. "Anyone you know?"

No one that immediately came to mind. These days she had no friends and only a very few acquaintances. Lenora hurried to the window and spotted the SUV.

"The minister, maybe?" Clayton asked.

"No. He's out of town all this week and gave me the keys to the church so I could let myself in."

Clayton glanced at her. Again, she couldn't see his eyes, but she figured there was displeasure lurking behind those dark shades. "Not wise. You're out here alone all by yourself."

That scolding put some starch in her posture. "I prefer working in solitude. Plus, I have a gun with me, and you know I can shoot." Then there was the whole part about her not trusting anyone. She figured trust would get her killed faster than going it alone.

"Good," Clayton mumbled, as if he hadn't actually heard what she said. Probably because his attention was fastened to the SUV.

No one got out of the vehicle. It just sat there with the front of it aimed right at them. It seemed menacing, but Lenora tried to assure herself that it could all be nothing. She'd gone three months without any contact with someone who wanted to hurt her. Of course, that was before Clayton had found her.

Had someone else found her, too?

Someone who'd hired another triggerman to finish the job that been started at the diner in Maverick Springs? Or maybe it'd even started before that, with Jill's murder.

Mercy, she needed answers.

"There's a back exit." She let him know in case they needed another way out.

"Yeah. It's locked from the inside. We might have to use it."

It shouldn't have surprised her that he knew about the locked exit. Clayton had no doubt scoped out the church before he'd come inside and surprised the heck out of her. So much for all her training. She hadn't even heard him skulking around the place.

"Neither lock will hold if someone wants to get inside," Clayton added. "Hand me the keys."

She riffled through her pocket and came up with them, and he jammed the key inside the internal deadbolt so the door was now double-locked. It was a good precaution to take, but the door was made of wood. Old wood at that. She doubted it would stand up to some hard kicks. There hadn't been a lot of need for security in this little country church.

Well, not before now, anyway.

The driver's side door of the SUV eased open, and in the same motion, Clayton drew his Glock. That put her heart right in her throat, and Lenora took out the small Smith & Wesson from the slide holster at the back waist of her jeans. It wasn't a comfortable fit anymore with her growing belly, but she was thankful that she'd decided to wear it anyway.

Clayton's mouth tightened. "If things go wrong here, I don't want you using that. I want you as far away from bullets as possible."

Lenora wanted that, too, along with wanting Clayton to be safe, but she had to be ready, too. She also had to keep hoping that this was just a false alarm, because the alternative was for her to accept that there was some kind of grand-scale conspiracy to murder her.

She held her breath and saw the man step from the driver's side of the SUV. Tall and lanky, he wore jeans and a dark shirt, common clothes for this part of the country, but it was the brown leather jacket that snagged her attention. It was nearly a hundred degrees outside, hardly jacket weather, which meant he was probably wearing it to conceal a weapon.

"I don't recognize him," she said before Clayton could ask. "Do you?"

"No."

That revved up her heart even more. She'd held out hope that their visitor was a lawman, maybe even the local sheriff. He sure had the lawman's look down pat— he glanced around, studying the entire grounds before his attention settled on the front of the church. However, Lenora saw no signs of a badge, but the guy was holding something.

A newspaper.

The man looked at the paper, then the church, as if comparing something. After a few moments, he tossed the newspaper back into the SUV.

Clayton took her by her left wrist and gently moved her behind him. No doubt trying to protect her. But he didn't move from the window.

Lenora stood there, watching the SUV driver from over Clayton's shoulder. Very close to him. So close that it stirred memories of him, and this was not a good time to be remembering anything about that night they'd slept together.

Some more movement got her mind back on the right track. The passenger's side door opened. A second man stepped out, and like the driver, he was also wearing a jacket.

Oh, mercy. Two of them and both likely armed. There was no way she could explain away this.

"Come on," Clayton said.

His grip on her wrist tightened, and with her in tow, he hurried through the rows of pews, past the pulpit and into the back entry. He didn't stop until they made it to the door.

There were no side windows next to the door, only

one on the west side of the building, facing the cemetery. Lenora did a quick look out, but didn't see Clayton's vehicle or anyone else on the grounds.

"Stay close and stay quiet," Clayton warned her.

Lenora would, as well as keep watch. But she also prayed that all of this was overkill.

He unlocked the door and stepped out ahead of her. Lenora didn't miss the grunt that he tried to muffle. Pained from the sun, no doubt. Still, he didn't let the pain or the sun slow him down. He eased her out behind him, shut the door, and they hurried toward the cemetery.

Clayton kept watch, too, his gaze firing all around them. There was a chain-link fence that surrounded the quarter acre or so of graves, and it was obviously meant to keep out deer rather than people, because there were no locks on the gate. He opened it and immediately pushed her behind a large angel headstone.

It wasn't her first choice of hiding place. In fact, the whole cemetery gave her the creeps. It reminded her of her father's grave, which she'd visited once—and only once—on the day she'd found out that he was dead. Lenora hoped they didn't have to stay crouched here for long.

She peered out and saw the men make their way toward the front of the church. They stopped by her car first, looked inside the windows and then continued to the front door. Because of the angle of the building, they disappeared from view. Maybe they would just knock and when no one answered, they'd leave.

But the thought had no sooner crossed her mind than Lenora heard something she didn't want to hear.

No knock.

There was a loud bashing sound, quickly followed

by a shot. Not in their direction, but the bullet made an unusual metallic sound.

Lenora knew exactly what it meant.

The men had shot through the lock on the front door and were no doubt already inside the church. It wouldn't take them but a minute or two to realize she wasn't there.

And they'd come looking for her.

"Let's move," Clayton ordered in a rough whisper. *"Now!"*

Chapter Five

Clayton waited a split second, until he was sure the two men were actually inside the church, and with his hand still gripping Lenora's wrist, he hurried across the cemetery.

"Stay low," he warned her.

She did, and he kept ducking them behind the larger tombstones, hoping that they'd become good cover if necessary. Most were marble, which should stop a bullet or two, but he didn't want to take the risk of a shot ricocheting and hitting Lenora.

Or him.

Because if he was out of the picture, it would leave her a sitting duck for whoever was inside the church. Yeah, she had a gun, and Clayton knew from the surveillance tapes of his own shooting that she was a good shot. However, those guys could be better.

Clayton took out his phone, and he made a whispered 9-1-1 call and gave the dispatcher their location. Maybe it wouldn't take long for the local authorities to respond, and even if it did, he had plans to get Lenora out of there anyway.

He cursed, not just over the fact that there were probably assassins mere yards away from them, but also that Lenora and his baby were right in the middle of the danger.

Again.

And worse, there was the possibility that he'd brought the danger right to Lenora. He hadn't been followed, he was sure of that, but obviously these men had found her, maybe the same way he had. He should have anticipated that would happen and gotten her away from the church the minute he showed up.

Of course, Lenora hadn't exactly cooperated with his demand that she leave with him. But Clayton was betting she'd cooperate now.

If they got out of this alive, that was.

He dragged her behind another tombstone that was closer to the far side fence and gate, and he listened and watched for any signs of the men. He also drew in some hard breaths, trying to fight off the pain that was stabbing through his head. The sunglasses helped, but nothing would help if he had to stay out in this blaring light too long. Not good. Because there was no way he could focus if the pain closed in on him.

Ironic, that a migraine could get them killed.

The pain and his plans to get her out of there did a short mental stutter, however, when he felt the movement against his back. He glanced over his shoulder at her to see what was going on.

"The baby" was all she said.

Oh.

He hadn't forgotten that she was pregnant, no way, but it was a jolt to feel his child moving around inside her. Once they were out of here, he really had to take some time to deal with everything he'd just learned.

"Where'd you park?" Her voice was shaky. She was

shaking, too, and her breathing was so fast that she might hyperventilate.

Clayton tipped his head to the other side of the cemetery, where the trees were thick. She wouldn't be able to see his truck, but it was there on an old ranch road about a fourth of a mile away.

He heard some bashing around in the church and figured the guys were tearing apart the place, looking for Lenora, but as long as they did that, they'd be inside. And they wouldn't be able to see Lenora and him. That was the cue he'd been waiting for. He hadn't wanted to run with her in the open, in case the men had plans to make a hasty exit from the church.

"Let's go," Clayton told Lenora.

They got moving again toward the gate, and even though his heartbeat was roaring in his ears, he heard something he didn't want to hear.

"There she is!" one of the men shouted.

Hell. Lenora and he had been spotted. Obviously it hadn't taken as long as Clayton had hoped for the men to search the church.

Clayton didn't look back, but he did position himself behind Lenora as he threw open the latch on the creaky metal gate and shoved her through it. He hated forcing her to run, but he didn't have a choice. And besides, there was a good chance they wouldn't even make it to his truck before these guys caught up with them.

With his left hand on her back, Clayton moved her through the small grassy clearing just outside the cemetery fence. They were just inches from the trees when he heard the shot blast through the air.

The sound blasted through him, too. It darn sure didn't help with the pain in his head. Didn't help Lenora, either, because her trembling got a heck of a lot worse.

Clayton resisted the urge to turn and fire. Instead he kept running, kept pushing Lenora until he could shove her behind one of the trees. It wasn't a second too soon, because another shot came their way.

He reminded her to stay low again, but he didn't stop except for just a brief moment. Too risky, even though the running could be a risk to the baby. They ran deeper into the clusters of trees, trying to put as much distance as possible between the men and them.

The next bullet tore through his shirtsleeve, grazing his arm. The knife-slice of pain was instant, but it didn't cause him to slow down. That's because the bullet had come way too close to Lenora.

He pushed her to the side, behind one of the larger trees, turned and saw the two men already in the cemetery. They were coming straight for Lenora and him.

Clayton took aim.

And fired.

The shot smacked into the taller man's shoulder, and even though Clayton was sure it wasn't a fatal strike, the man dropped to the ground.

Another shot sounded—a loud, thick blast. Not fired by one of the men, but rather by Lenora. From the corner of his eye, Clayton saw that she was leaning out from the opposite side the tree, and she still had her gun aimed.

The second man fell to the ground, too, but Clayton didn't think Lenora's bullet had actually hit him. The gunman just seemed to be getting out of the way. Maybe neither of the men had thought that Lenora would actually return fire. Clayton had thought that, too, because he'd made it pretty clear he didn't want her to take any unnecessary chances.

He didn't waste time warning her to stay down and quit taking chances, because they only had a few seconds before those men got back on their feet. Clayton took hold of her wrist and got her moving toward his truck.

It wasn't long before he heard a welcome sound. Sirens. A much faster response than Clayton had estimated, and maybe it would send the men running back to their SUV. He wanted to arrest them. Question them, too. But maybe the locals would do that while he got Lenora out of there.

"They're not following us," Lenora said, looking over her shoulder.

Good. Just a few more yards and they'd be one step closer to safety.

Clayton shoved aside a low-hanging tree branch and they threaded their way through some underbrush to the trail. The truck was still there, thank God, and he threw open the door and practically pushed Lenora into the passenger's seat. He crawled around her so he could start the engine and he slammed on the accelerator.

"Put on your seat belt," he told her, doing the same while trying to keep watch all around them.

The trail was just that—a trail—filled with bumps and holes. That made for a bumpy ride, but it wasn't their discomfort that concerned him most. There were plenty of trees between the cemetery and the trail, and if the gunmen decided to outrun the law, they could come through those trees and start shooting.

Clayton wanted to figure out what they were after. And why.

There she is.

That was what the man had shouted when he'd spotted them in the cemetery.

She.

Did that mean they were looking only for Lenora

and not him? It was something he needed to consider. Especially after everything Lenora had told him about her life as a criminal informant.

That was the last thing he'd expected from her.

Here he'd had her in his protective custody, and it'd all been a ruse for a deep-cover operation. Once he got Lenora to safety, he was going to make some calls to let his own boss and Lenora's task-force leader know that he wasn't happy about playing the dupe, since his life had been on the line, too.

He hated lies.

They were something his worthless father, Melvin Larson, had manipulated him with countless times. But Clayton pushed that old wound aside and kept maneuvering the truck through the trail.

The trees were so close in spots that the branches scraped against the sides of his truck and the rocks battered against the undercarriage. The sound was practically deafening, but Clayton tried to pick through it so he could figure out what was going on.

He could still make out the sirens. That was good. And he figured they were headed for the church. However, he wasn't sure from which direction the locals would arrive. It was possible he would pass them when he made it to the road.

"I need you to make a call," Clayton said, handing his phone to Lenora. "Call my brother Dallas. It's the first number in my contacts. And ask him to run the plates of that SUV." He gave her the license-plate number and hoped knowing who owned the vehicle would also help them identify who'd just taken shots at them.

Lenora made the call and was still in the process of trying to explain to Dallas what was going on when Clayton spotted the road just ahead. He slowed, bringing his truck almost to a stop, and he saw the other vehicle flying up the road toward them.

Not a police cruiser.

But the SUV that their attackers had driven.

Since those men would definitely see his truck and maybe attempt to block their escape, Clayton had to do something fast. He damn sure didn't want to have to drive in Reverse on the trail. Not with a pair of assassins bearing down on them. Besides, even if he could manage to outrun them, eventually the trail would end and Lenora and he would be trapped.

Clayton slammed on the accelerator and bolted out onto the road. The SUV hit its brakes. Not for long, though. It only took a few moments before the driver readjusted and came right after them.

"Get down," Clayton told Lenora, but he didn't wait for her to do that. He pushed her down onto the seat. "Tell Dallas we're traveling east on the farm road outside of Sadler's Falls. We have two men in pursuit, and I need the locals out here now. These men are armed and dangerous."

He hadn't thought it possible, but her voice was even shakier now. She managed to tell Dallas what he needed to know and then pressed the end button.

"Dallas says he's on it," she relayed to Clayton.

Clayton didn't doubt it. Dallas would immediately call the locals and send them in this direction. He only hoped it'd be soon and that their attackers wouldn't start shooting again. It was hard to be accurate shooting from a moving vehicle, but he didn't want one of these SOBs getting off a lucky shot.

"Hang on," Clayton warned her, a split second before he went into a sharp curve.

He had to fight to keep control of the truck, and the

right tires dug into the dirt and gravel shoulder. Another round of rocks battered against his truck, and it sounded like gunfire.

"Oh, God," Lenora said, and she started to lift her head.

"Stay down," he warned her. "They're not shooting."

That obviously didn't steady her nerves, and while still repeating *oh, God,* she put her hands over her belly. Protecting the baby. From what Lenora had told him she was a trained agent, but there wasn't enough training in the world to stay unrattled while your unborn baby was in danger. Even though he'd only learned about his fatherhood just minutes earlier, he was feeling the same thing.

Clayton went into another sharp turn just as the SUV accelerated, and it slammed into the back of his truck. The jolt caused a whiplash effect, with his body jolting forward, then back, and Clayton tossed his gun on the seat so he could use both hands on the steering wheel.

"I'll keep watch," Lenora insisted.

And even though he didn't want her to do it, she levered herself up a little and fastened her attention on the side window. She also lifted her gun, getting it ready. There was no way Clayton would let her lean out the window and return fire, and that meant he had to do something now to defuse this mess of a situation.

He saw the sign for Sadler's Falls ahead, and without slowing as much as he should have, he took the turn on what had to be two tires at most. The truck wobbled, but he immediately corrected and got control.

Behind them, the SUV squealed to a stop.

Clayton didn't take the time to figure out why the driver had done that. He put the pedal to the metal and got Lenora out of there.

Chapter Six

Lenora kept her attention plastered to the side mirror. It'd been nearly an hour and a half since she'd last seen the two gunmen in the SUV, but she wasn't taking any more chances. She'd already made enough stupid mistakes, and she couldn't afford to make more.

Even though that might be exactly what she was doing now.

That's because Clayton had insisted on driving them to his family's ranch, which she estimated was now only a few miles away. She figured with six marshals living there the place was safe enough, but she hadn't wanted to bring the danger to Clayton's doorstep.

Soon, very soon, she'd need to make arrangements to leave Maverick County. The state. Heck, maybe even the country.

"Dead end," Clayton mumbled when he finished his latest call to his brother.

Lenora had lost count of how many phone conversations there had been, all with his marshal brothers, but so far none of the calls had given Clayton and her any good news. This one didn't sound any better.

From one of the calls, they'd learned that by the time the cops from Sadler's Falls had made it to the farm road, the gunmen in the SUV had been nowhere in sight, and even a makeshift roadblock had failed to rein them in. Worse, recovering their spent shell casings from the woods and cemetery would probably turn out to be a needle-in-a-haystack search.

"The license plates on the SUV didn't pan out," Clayton relayed to her. "They were fake."

Of course they were. Every indication was that these guys were pros, and they wouldn't have made the mistake of using a vehicle that could be traced back to them or the person who'd hired them. Still, she'd hoped Clayton and she would get lucky.

"Dallas thinks he's figured out how these guys found you," Clayton added. "Apparently, the Sadler's Falls newspaper ran a front-page article about the restoration of the stained-glass windows at the church. In addition to being printed and circulated, the story was posted on the newspaper's online site."

"But I used a fake name." However, Lenora immediately realized that didn't matter. "These guys had probably scoured the web, looking for anything to do with stained-glass restoration." And the article had led them to her.

Yet another mistake on her part.

She shouldn't have taken work doing any restoration, especially not in such a small town, where she couldn't just blend in.

"These gunmen obviously used the same approach I did to find you," Clayton reminded her. "That's why you need to be someplace where I can keep you safe."

In his mind, that someplace safe was the ranch.

"I really don't like the idea of coming here," she said again.

Again, he just seemed to ignore her, and he glanced at her stomach. "Are you okay?"

It wasn't the first time he'd asked that, and Lenora nodded as she'd done before. To say she was okay would be a lie, but that was only because her nerves were frazzled and she was exhausted. She hadn't been hurt, and she knew the baby was fine because he or she was kicking like crazy.

She considered plopping Clayton's hands on her belly so he could feel those kicks as proof that the baby was truly okay, but that seemed almost intimate. Strange, considering they'd had sex, but he didn't remember that one-night stand, and reminding him of it probably wasn't a good idea. Not when she was trying to keep some emotional and physical distance between them.

"I guess it's occurred to you that both attacks have come when we've been together," she tossed out there. "And that's a good reason for me not to be at the ranch. I don't want anyone in your family hurt because of me."

He turned off the main highway and onto a two-lane road. "That baby is part of my family."

Oh, mercy. That sounded territorial, and while it was true that the baby was his, Clayton was in no shape for fatherhood. He'd been sharp and efficient when making the wrap-up calls about this latest shooting, but his bunched-up forehead let her know that he was in pain. Probably a heck of a lot more pain than he'd ever be willing to admit.

"Are *you* okay?" she asked, repeating his question.

That caused him to scowl, but then he winced at making the simple facial gesture. The pain was obviously getting worse.

He reached over, threw open the glove compartment and took out a prescription bottle. He shoved two pills into his mouth, gulped some water from the bottle on the console between them and threw the meds back in the glove compartment.

"I can drive," she offered.

When he didn't answer her, she grabbed some tissues from beneath his meds, wet them with water and pressed it to the back of his neck. At first he flinched as if he might push her hand away, but then he mumbled a thanks.

"My mother had migraines," she explained. "She said a cool cloth helped sometimes."

"It does," he agreed a moment later. "But what'll help more is to find the person responsible for these attacks."

She had to agree with that, but so far they had zero leads. Well, except the most obvious one—Clayton and her.

"There's only one motive I can think of as to why we've been attacked twice. Someone wants to eliminate us as witnesses to Jill's murder. Without us, maybe Riggs's lawyers might feel they can manipulate the evidence to get the charges reduced or dismissed."

He made a sound of agreement. "So, Riggs maybe hired someone, but he would have needed help to orchestrate an attack like this. And I don't mean just money kind of help. He'd need someone he could trust on the outside to do the legwork."

Clayton took another turn onto an even narrower road, and she saw the sign for the Blue Creek Ranch. Clayton's home.

Lenora shifted the wet tissues a little, and her fingers grazed the back of his neck. Clayton didn't move, but he made another sound that might have been a grunt of pain.

But she rethought that.

Even though she couldn't see his eyes behind those

shades, the breath that left his mouth wasn't of pain, but of discomfort.

Maybe it was this blasted attraction that still seemed to be between them. He probably wasn't any more comfortable with it than she was. However, that didn't make it go away.

"Any ideas who Riggs could have hired?" she asked, forcing her thoughts back on the only subject that she should be thinking about—this investigation.

"No one immediately comes to mind. What about you? Any ideas?"

"Yes," she had to answer. "The task-force leader, James Britt. I told you that his behavior after your shooting was suspicious."

"You didn't talk to him about it?" Clayton immediately wanted to know. The concern was in his voice now, probably because he was worried that she'd tipped her hand and let James think she believed he was doing something illegal.

"No. In fact, I haven't spoken to him since your shooting. He thinks I left the justice department because I was shaken by Jill's murder. I was," she added in a mumble.

"Yeah." That's all he said, but it was obvious from his expression he was thinking about it. She'd also slept with Clayton because she'd been *shaken*.

Lenora quickly moved on to something else that didn't involve memories of sex with Clayton. "What about Corey Dayton, the gunman I shot at the diner? Did anything turn up on who might have hired him?" Because that could lead them back to Riggs.

"Nothing so far, but I need to take a harder look at everything. That includes a chat with the prison officials where Riggs is being held. I want to know who he's had communications with. I need to check out his lawyers, too."

Yes, a lot of work ahead, but first she had to deal with what else lay ahead. *Literally.* She looked out at the sprawling pastures and equally sprawling ranch house at the end of the road. In addition to hundreds of Angus cows, there were also about a half dozen ranch hands milling around and doing various chores.

"My foster father came from money," Clayton offered, maybe because she seemed so shocked by the sheer size of the place. "But he was first and foremost a lawman."

A marshal, she recalled from the background check she'd read on Clayton. Now retired, Kirby Granger had rescued not only Clayton but five other boys from the Rocky Creek Children's Facility.

Clayton tipped his head to an older wood frame house near the front of the pasture. "My brother Harlan lives there. You remember meeting him."

Yes, he'd given her the third degree about why she was visiting Clayton while they rode in the ambulance to the hospital. Lenora was pretty sure that Harlan didn't like her much.

He pointed to another place, not nearly as large as the main ranch house. A one-story that looked to be recently built. "My brother Dallas and his fiancée, Joelle, live there. You probably won't see much of Joelle while you're here. She's finishing up her job in Austin, but she'll move here for good in a month or two and work for the D.A."

A big family and it was getting bigger. The baby would add to that, and it was a reminder that all the marshals on the Blue Creek Ranch might want to be part of not just the baby's life but her own.

Not exactly a settling thought.

She'd spent years being private. Secretive. An out-and-out liar on occasion. Now she was about to be under the same roof with people devoted to upholding the law.

Clayton pulled to a stop in the circular drive in front of the main house. Lenora was so caught up in looking at the grounds, pastures and sheer size of the place that it took her several seconds to notice the man and woman seated in the white rockers on the porch, which stretched all the way across the front of the house. The woman was in her late fifties or early sixties, with a sturdy build and graying auburn hair. The man was younger, mid-thirties, and he wore a white Stetson, starched white shirt and jeans.

"What the hell?" Clayton mumbled. Judging from his frown, these were not people he wanted to see.

"I told him it wasn't a good time," the woman said, getting to her feet the moment Clayton and Lenora stepped from the truck. She was frowning until her gaze landed on Lenora—specifically on her stomach— and the frown shifted to a puzzling glance at Clayton.

"Lenora, this is Stella Doyle, a friend of the family."

Clayton's introduction had some frost to it, but Lenora didn't think it was aimed at Stella, but rather at the man. When he stood from the rocker, Lenora saw the badge pinned to his chest. Not a marshal—a Texas Ranger.

"Ranger Griffin Morris," the man introduced himself. He extended his hand, but Clayton didn't shake it. "I understand you had some trouble over in Sadler's Falls. Is the sheriff handling that?"

"A lot of us are handling that," Clayton grumbled. "At least we were before I had to stop to talk to you."

"He wanted to come in," Stella explained, her mouth

tight, "but I told him it wasn't a good time, that you two had just got shot at." Her gaze softened. "Are you all right?"

"Fine," Clayton snarled, and Lenora settled for a nod.

"He's got a headache," Lenora said to no one in particular and she wadded up the wet tissues that she'd held to the back of his neck.

"Even more reason this isn't a good time," Stella mumbled. Obviously, she wasn't any happier about the Ranger's presence than Clayton, so that probably meant he wasn't here about the shooting.

"Where are Kirby and the others?" Clayton asked Stella. He went up the steps and onto the porch, out of the direct sunlight.

Stella hitched her thumb toward the door. "Kirby's in his room, recovering from the radiation treatment he got today. The nurse is with him. Your brothers are all out working on finding those men who shot at you." She looked at Lenora then. "Kirby has cancer and is bad off. Might not make it, but Ranger Morris here didn't seem to understand that this isn't a good time for a visit."

Oh, Lenora figured he understood all right, but obviously he had some official reason for being here. A critical reason. Because if he hadn't, Stella would have probably already managed to send him on his way.

"I'll handle this," Clayton told Stella. "Why don't you go ahead and take Lenora inside while I talk to the Ranger."

Stella aimed a huff at Ranger Morris and motioned for Lenora to follow her. "I'll be inside in a minute," Lenora explained to the woman. First, she wanted to make sure this visit had nothing to do with everything else going on, and if it did, she was staying to hear what Morris had to say.

The Ranger volleyed glances between Clayton and her as if he was checking with Clayton to make sure it was all right for her to be there.

"You're here about Jonah Webb," Clayton said to the Ranger. So, not about the shooting, but Clayton didn't seem to be shutting her out of the conversation.

Lenora remembered hearing that the body of a man had been found several months earlier. Jonah Webb. He'd been head of the children's home where Clayton was raised. It'd been a nightmare of a place, from all accounts, and Webb had been responsible for most of the bad stuff that'd gone on there.

"I remember reading that Webb's killer was caught," she said to the Ranger.

Morris nodded. "His wife, Sarah, confessed to the crime, but we have a lot of evidence to indicate that she didn't act alone. She's not a large woman, and someone would have almost certainly had to help her move the body from the second floor of the building and then bury it."

Oh, mercy. Did the Rangers think Clayton had done that? "Did Sarah Webb name an accomplice?"

He shook his head. "And she's in a coma. She's been that way since she was shot three months ago."

By Clayton's foster brother Dallas. Lenora had read all those details, too. Dallas had been forced to shoot the woman when she tried to kill him and his soon-to-be wife, Joelle.

"I wanted Webb dead," Clayton volunteered. "But I didn't help Sarah kill him or dispose of the body. And no one else in my family did, either."

Ranger Morris didn't have a reaction to that and looked at the notepad he pulled from his pocket. "I saw in your medical records from Rocky Creek that you were running a fever the night Webb disappeared."

"One hundred two degrees," Clayton confirmed. "I slept through the night."

"So a couple of your brothers said." Morris drew in a long breath. "I guess you see the problem with that. All of you are each other's alibis, but we know that Sarah had an accomplice who either lived in the facility or had access to it."

"There were plenty of other kids living in that place," Clayton explained. "I hope you're looking as hard at them as you are at me and my brothers."

"I am." Morris paused. "And, of course, I'm looking into your father, too."

"Kirby had nothing to do with this," Clayton snapped.

He glanced at his notes again. "That's the identical comment I got from all your brothers."

"Because it's not just a *comment,* it's the truth." Clayton didn't hesitate.

The Ranger made a sound that could have meant anything. "I have to put this in my report, so I need to know if you saw or heard anything suspicious the night that Webb disappeared."

"Nothing." Again, no hesitation, but this time Clayton opened the door. "I need to get Lenora off her feet," he added, and it had a definite goodbye tone.

Ranger Morris looked as if he wanted to demand that the interview continue, but Lenora slid her hand over her stomach. She wasn't hurting, the baby had even stopped kicking, but she figured it would get Morris to back off.

It did.

He tipped his hat. "I'll be in touch with you soon," Morris assured him, and he walked off the porch toward a dark blue truck.

Clayton didn't waste any time. He got her inside and shut the door, locked it, but he didn't go far. He stopped and leaned the back of his head against the glass insert on the door.

"How bad is the headache?" she asked in a whisper. Lenora eased off his Stetson and put it on a peg hook next to the door. "And before you answer, I'd prefer the truth."

"I've had worse," he mumbled.

She was afraid that was indeed the truth, and it was a stark reminder that Clayton wouldn't be going through this if it wasn't for her. She was the reason he'd been shot in the first place.

Lenora pressed the wet tissues against his neck again. This time, the front. "Do the doctors have any idea how much longer you'll get the headaches?"

He pulled off his glasses, hooked them on his jeans pocket and met her gaze. "They're getting farther apart."

She stared at him. "Do you do that a lot—dodge questions that you don't want to answer?"

He made another of those noncommittal sounds, obviously still not planning to answer. That meant he might be dealing with these for the rest of his life.

The glass panel on the door made this part of the entry light, so Lenora took him by the arm and led him into the dark room on the right. It was a den with brown leather furniture, but thankfully all the blinds were closed on the row of windows on the far wall. Since she doubted that she could convince him to sit, Lenora put him back against the wall and continued to put the wet tissues on his throat.

"I'm fine," he mumbled and would have moved away from her if she hadn't blocked him with her body.

It didn't take her long to realize that just wasn't a

good idea. Her breasts landed against his chest, and the close contact gave her another jolting reminder that Clayton was, well, hot. She'd thought it the first time she laid eyes on him, and apparently her body wasn't about to reverse that opinion now.

She tried to step back, but this time it was Clayton who did the stopping. He snagged her by the wrist before she could put some distance between them. Lenora was about to tell him it wasn't a good idea, but then she saw something other than pain in his deep-brown eyes. The heat, yes.

But maybe more.

"Do you remember?" she asked. She didn't clarify—did he remember having sex with her—but Lenora figured they were on the same page here.

Their bodies seemed to be, anyway.

The air between them changed. So did the rhythm of her breathing. And even though she tried to level it, Lenora was reasonably sure she was giving off every signal a woman could give to a man to let him know she was *interested*. Definitely not a good idea, because she needed to get away from Clayton so he wouldn't be attacked again.

It was a solid reason to move.

But she didn't.

She huffed, beyond frustrated with herself. And worse. She still didn't back away when Clayton leaned down, his mouth inching toward hers.

"This might help me remember." His warm breath hit against her lips when he spoke.

And suddenly more than anything, Lenora wanted him to remember. Oh, and she wanted him to kiss her, too. Clayton might not have any memories of their one-night stand, but Lenora was well aware that he could set fires with his mouth.

He moved in closer. Closer. And she was just a breath away from kissing him again. Too bad she could already feel it and also too bad her body seemed to think this was foreplay, that Clayton would haul her off to bed again.

That wouldn't happen.

Even if she desperately wanted it.

Her eyelids were already fluttering down, getting ready for that kiss, when Clayton stopped. It took her a moment to realize why. The baby was kicking, and with her body pressed against Clayton's, he could feel it.

In that split second of time, the heat went from his eyes, and he slid his hand over her belly. Concern replaced the heat and the pain.

"Is the baby okay?" he asked.

It took her a moment to switch gears, and Lenora pushed away the attraction that she shouldn't be feeling anyway. Especially not a time like this. "She's fine."

Clayton blinked. "She?"

Lenora shook her head when she realized what he was thinking. "I've had ultrasounds, but I was still trying to make up my mind about knowing the sex of the baby. So the tech didn't tell me."

His forehead bunched up again. "You went through the trauma of the shooting when you were…what…just two months pregnant? Are you sure that didn't harm the baby in some way?"

"Positive. I had a checkup just last week."

That didn't ease the tension in his face. "And you need another one after what happened today." He cursed again. "I should have already thought of it. Hell, I should have already taken you to the doctor."

Lenora was about to assure him that she would indeed see her doctor as soon as she left the ranch, but Clayton pulled out his phone, scrolled through the numbers and made a call.

"Dr. Landry," he said, then paused. "No, it's not about Kirby. I need you to come out to the ranch, though. To examine someone." He paused. "A pregnant woman in her second trimester." Another pause, and he looked at her. "Are you having cramps or anything?"

"No," Lenora quickly answered. She wanted to grab the phone and tell the doctor this wasn't necessary.

But what if it was?

Lenora stepped back and tried not to think of the worst-case scenario, but she did anyway. She couldn't lose this baby. And it certainly wouldn't hurt to have a doctor check her out while she was making arrangements to leave and go someplace else.

"Dr. Landry's on the way," Clayton relayed to her as soon as he ended the call. "She's not an obstetrician, but she does deliver some babies as part of her family practice."

Before the last word had even left his mouth, Lenora heard the sound of a vehicle pulling to a stop in front of the ranch house. Normally, a sound that ordinary wouldn't have shot renewed concern through her, but after the day Clayton and she had had, nothing felt normal and safe.

"You expecting anyone?" she asked.

"Maybe Ranger Griffin came back for round two."

Clayton shoved back on his sunglasses and hurried to the door so he could look out the glass panel. He cursed.

Lenora hurried to his side, looked out at the visitor who'd just stepped from a black car, and she mumbled some profanity, too. This was not someone she wanted to see at the ranch. Not so soon after the latest attack.

James Britt, the head of the task force to which she'd once been assigned. Her handler. He was also her top suspect in these murder attempts.

With his hand over his gun, their suspect was making a beeline for the front door.

Chapter Seven

Clayton recognized the tall, dark-haired man walking up the porch steps. They'd met briefly when Clayton had been assigned to protect Lenora and Jill. Of course, at the time he hadn't known that James was Lenora's boss.

"I'll take care of this," Lenora insisted, and she might have tried to do just that if Clayton hadn't caught her by the hand and forced her to stay put.

No way was he letting her go out there.

Clayton wasn't ready for a confrontation with a man who might be working for the killer, Riggs. Not yet, anyway. First he wanted Lenora checked out with the doctor and then moved to someplace safe. But with James on his doorstep, Clayton decided to go ahead and question the man.

While Lenora stayed inside, that was.

The doorbell rang, but Clayton ignored it and phoned his brother Harlan. "I got a visitor," Clayton explained. "Special Agent James Britt. I need a fast background check and let me know ASAP if you see any red flags on this guy."

"You think he's somehow connected to the shooting?" Harlan asked.

"At a minimum. He could be connected to Riggs."

Harlan mumbled some profanity. "I'll send Wyatt out

there to the ranch while I work on this. He'll get there as fast as he can. I'll also make sure a few of the ranch hands move closer to the house."

Clayton didn't refuse the backup, but he hoped it wouldn't be needed.

"I've been looking deeper into Lenora's background," Harlan continued. "And before you blast me out of the water for doing that, just hear me out. Something's not adding up about her, and I want to know what it is."

Yeah, it was *something,* all right. "She has a connection with Agent Britt. She worked for him on the task force that investigated Riggs." It wasn't the whole story, not by any means, but it would have to do for now, because the doorbell rang again.

"How long have you known this about her?" Harlan snapped.

"Not nearly long enough." He'd give Harlan more details later, but it wasn't exactly comfortable talking about her criminal past with his family. That didn't mean Harlan wouldn't find it on his own.

"Wait here," Clayton told Lenora when he ended the call with Harlan. The doorbell rang yet again, and it was followed by a heavy knock.

She didn't listen to him. In fact, Lenora moved in front of him when he reached to open the door. "I know the right questions to ask him, and it could lead to his arrest. If I talk to him, it could end the danger right here."

That was the only thing she could have said that would have made him think twice about letting her in on this impromptu interrogation.

But Clayton did think twice.

And after doing that, he still shook his head. Ending the danger *right here* could put Lenora in the middle of something that he wanted her and the baby to avoid.

He glanced out again and saw the two ranch hands making their way toward the house. Both were armed with rifles, probably on Harlan's orders. Good. It might be overkill, but Clayton welcomed it. If Agent Britt was dirty, he likely wouldn't start any trouble with three guns ready to return that trouble.

"Stay behind me," Clayton said to her as a way of compromising. "If anything goes wrong, I want you to get out of the way fast."

She didn't argue, maybe because she knew it was a huge concession that he'd just given her, but she did draw her gun from the back of her jeans. Clayton drew his gun as well, and he opened the door only a few inches, keeping his weapon out of sight but ready.

"Marshal Caldwell," James immediately greeted him. He glanced back at the two armed ranch hands, and his scowl deepened.

"Agent Britt," Clayton replied in the same crisp tone. "To put it mildly, the timing of your visit is suspicious, so why are you here?"

Despite the direct question, James didn't answer right away. His gaze went from Clayton's sunglasses to the scar on his forehead, and then to Lenora, who was peering over his shoulder.

"I heard about the APB out for the two thugs who took shots at you," James finally said. The chilly tone of his voice came through in the equally chilly glance he gave her. Maybe a dismissal. Maybe anger. It was hard to tell. "Also heard the shooting involved a stained-glass restorer, and I figured that could only mean one thing. *Lenora.* Guess I figured right."

"That still doesn't explain why you came here," Lenora quickly pointed out.

James huffed as if the answer was obvious and

planted his hands on his hips. "Just because you ended your association with the justice department, it doesn't mean I forgot about caring what happened to you." He glanced away, cursed. "I feel bad about Jill's murder and everything that you've been through since."

"But you didn't feel bad enough to return my calls for days after Jill's death and Clayton's shooting."

James's jaw tightened. Clearly he didn't like what Lenora had said, but judging from the glare the agent gave him, he believed that Clayton was somehow responsible for Lenora speaking her mind.

"There was a glitch in communication that night," James explained. "I didn't get your message for hours, and then I got word from another agent that you were in the marshal's hotel room. Where you spent most of the night. I was trying to figure out how to handle it."

That didn't sit well with Clayton, and he did some glaring of his own. "Why would you believe that you needed to handle anything? Lenora and I were both consenting adults, and by then she was no longer in my protective custody."

"Lenora wasn't exactly thinking straight that night, and I didn't want her breaking down and revealing her real identity to you. It might have compromised the entire task force."

Even though Clayton didn't like that answer, either, he glanced back at Lenora to see what she thought of it. She clearly wasn't buying it.

"If you were concerned that I'd spill all to Clayton, then why not return my calls and warn me not to do it?" she pressed.

Another huff from James. "Because I was trying to figure out how to deal with it. Besides, I was pretty torn up about Jill's murder, too. I needed some time to work out things in my head."

Lenora stepped out next to Clayton. He groaned and shot her a stern warning to step back, but she obviously couldn't see the look behind his glasses. If it wouldn't have caused a full-blown migraine, he would have shed the shades just so she could see that he did *not* want her to do this. Of course, she already knew, so the migraine would just be wasted.

It didn't take long for James's gaze to drop to her stomach. "You're pregnant." He didn't seem exactly surprised, but upset instead. "You should have let me know something like that."

"Well, you and I haven't exactly stayed in touch, have we?" Lenora clearly didn't try to take the sarcasm from her voice.

"Are you accusing me of something?" James fired back.

"Are you guilty of something?" she returned just as fast.

James didn't answer her, but instead turned back to Clayton. "I know you're looking for the person responsible for putting a bullet in your head, but it wasn't me. I'm not even convinced it was Riggs."

Clayton hadn't expected James to say that. "Riggs has a solid motive. Or at least he believes he does. He could want Lenora and me out of the way so we can't testify against him."

"Even without your testimony, he'll be convicted," James reminded him. "Lenora and you have both done affidavits, and your sworn testimony could be used against him. Riggs and his lawyers know that."

True. However, there was the other angle that Lenora and Clayton had already considered. "But with us out of the way, maybe Riggs could get murder one reduced to a lesser charge."

James didn't argue that, but his attention went from Clayton to Lenora. "I've been investigating this, and I think we need to take a harder look at Quentin Hewitt."

Because Lenora's arm was against his, Clayton felt her muscles tense, and despite the shades, he saw some of the color drain from her face.

"Quentin was the man who got me involved in money laundering," she said, her voice barely louder than a whisper. Clearly, she wasn't comfortable talking about this. Clayton wasn't comfortable hearing it, either, but from the sound of it, this could be critical.

"Why would this guy want to shoot us?" Clayton asked James.

James, however, looked at Lenora. "You want me to tell him, or should you?" And for some reason, the agent didn't seem too upset about revealing something that was obviously unsettling to Lenora.

Yet another reason to dislike the man.

Lenora didn't dodge Clayton's gaze. She looked him straight in the eyes. "Five years ago, I was Quentin's executive assistant. And I was in love with him. Or I thought I was, anyway. I did whatever he wanted me to do to make his business succeed."

So, Quentin and she had likely been lovers. Clayton had to push aside the quick jolt of jealousy he felt and remind himself that it'd happened well before he met her. And besides, it wasn't as if he and Lenora were involved except for the baby. A one-night stand didn't make a real relationship even when it made a real baby.

"Quentin was the initial target of our investigation," James continued when she didn't. "Lenora helped us find evidence against him, without his knowledge, of course. We led Quentin to believe we got the dirt against him from other sources. So that he could avoid jail time, he in turn helped us convict at least a half dozen big-time criminals. Afterward, Lenora stayed on the task force, again without Quentin's knowledge, and he went into WITSEC."

Witness Security Program.

Ironically, it was run by the U.S. Marshals Service. Of course, Clayton wouldn't automatically have been told of anyone entering the program, and even if he had been in this case, the name would have meant nothing to him. He certainly wouldn't have connected it to Lenora.

"Quentin went missing from WITSEC just a couple of days after Jill was murdered," James added.

Clayton didn't like that timing any more than he did the timing of this visit or the attack at the church. "Maybe he's dead."

The agent shook his head. "I have three confirmed sightings of him. No, Quentin's very much alive, and I think he saw or heard something that made him realize Lenora had been working for the justice department."

She groaned softly. "Quentin could have done those break-ins at my house that happened before your shooting." Tears sprang to her eyes. "Clayton, I'm so sorry. I should have never visited you that day."

Lenora still had a grip on the gun she was holding, but her hand dropped limply to her side, and she turned and went back inside the house.

Clayton didn't want her to be alone, especially after seeing those tears, but he needed just a little more from James. "You consider Quentin dangerous?"

"Oh, yes. He's in love with Lenora. The only way we convinced him to go into WITSEC and keep his distance from her was because we led him to believe that it'd keep her safe. We convinced him that the cronies he put in prison might try to use her for revenge to get back at him."

And all of that would have come crashing down if Quentin had learned that Lenora had been the very informant who'd turned him over to the authorities in the first place.

Yeah, that was a big motive for murder, all right.

"If Quentin's behind this," James continued, "you could be an innocent bystander in both of the shootings."

There she is.

That's what the two gunmen at the church had said, so maybe they were indeed just looking for Lenora. It didn't change things. It only meant Clayton had to do a better job of protecting her.

"I'll send you the file I have on Quentin," James volunteered. "And I'd like to offer Lenora a safe house until we work out this mess."

"Yes to the file," Clayton agreed. "No to the safe house. I'll work out security for her."

James nodded. "Figured you would. Just know that we're on the same side here."

Clayton wasn't a hundred percent convinced of that. James could be trying to use Quentin to throw suspicion off himself, and that was something Clayton would investigate further.

They both looked at the truck that was practically flying up the road toward the house. It was Wyatt, and even though there didn't seem to be an eminent threat, Clayton was glad he was here. Wyatt slammed on the brakes and got out the moment the truck stopped.

"One of your marshal brothers, I assume," James said, clearly not happy about the security measures they were taking for his visit. "I'll send you that report on

Quentin." And with that, he walked back to his car, passing a hard look at Wyatt along the way.

"He's the guy who hired someone to take shots at you?" Wyatt asked, and he didn't wait until James was out of earshot, either.

"Maybe. I need you to make sure he leaves the ranch. I have to talk to Lenora."

Wyatt pinned his attention to James, who started his car and pulled away. "Harlan told me she's pregnant."

"Yeah. The baby's mine."

It wasn't surprise, exactly, that went through Wyatt's eyes. Envy, maybe. Now that he was a widower, Wyatt was again the hot catch of Maverick Springs. The one all the single women wanted. A few married ones, too. But Clayton knew that this particular hot catch wanted to be a father, and he wanted it bad. So far there hadn't been any baby reminders at the ranch, but there would be now.

Well, there would be if Clayton could keep Lenora safe and somehow convince her not to run out of his life again.

"See to Lenora," Wyatt said, his jaw muscles stirring. "I'll make sure the potential scum isn't a threat."

Clayton went back inside, welcoming both the semidarkness and the A/C. There was sweat trickling down his neck, and his mind was racing with all the things he had to do. First on his list, though, was Lenora.

She wasn't in the entry, where he'd expected her to be waiting, so Clayton checked the den. Not there, either. He went through the formal dining room and into the kitchen, where Stella was seated at the table.

"She's out there," Stella volunteered, pointing to the sunroom that stretched across the side of the house. The worst place possible for him because of the light. Stella had added heavy blinds and drapes to the other rooms in the house, but the sunroom had been left as it was.

Clayton took a deep breath, walked out to the sunroom and found her seated in a white wicker chair.

She was crying.

The second she spotted Clayton, however, Lenora swiped away the tears, jumped to her feet and went to him. She backed him out of the bright light and into the laundry room off the kitchen. The overhead light was on there, but she slapped it off.

"I'm so sorry, Clayton."

Hell. He didn't want an apology. He took off his glasses, hooked his arm around her waist and pulled her to him. "We don't even know if Quentin had any part in this. Everything's speculation at this point."

Well, everything except that she felt pretty darn good in his arms. He didn't need any more reminders of why the two of them had landed in bed, but he got one anyway.

A short reminder, because she pulled away from him.

"I need to leave, to put some distance between us," she whispered.

He would have bet a year's salary she would say that. "Not a chance. Again, no guarantees that you and you alone are the target. If we're not together, it might make it easier for someone to pick us off."

Harsh but true.

"Plus, there's the baby," Clayton continued. "I want to protect him or her. And don't start talking about how I don't remember you, how I don't remember the night the baby was conceived. That doesn't matter."

"Of course it does. I read your background, Clayton, and there's nothing in it to indicate you ever considered having children."

"True," he readily admitted. "I didn't exactly have a stellar childhood, so it didn't make me eager to be a father."

Even though it was dark and he could barely see her expression, Clayton figured he hadn't convinced her.

Nope.

She'd run first chance she got. But before he could try to say something else that would prevent her from running, his phone buzzed, and when he saw Harlan's name on the screen, he knew it was a call he should take.

"This conversation isn't over," Clayton told her, and he pushed the answer button. "Please tell me you have good news, Harlan."

"Well, it's news. Don't know how good it is, though. I just had an interesting conversation with a friend who's an FBI agent and did a lot of deep-cover work. He cut through some red tape and got us fast answers about Agent James Britt."

Good. It was exactly what they needed. Clayton put the call on speaker so that Lenora could hear. "*We're* listening," he said to alert his brother this was no longer a private conversation.

Harlan hesitated a couple of moments. "I'm not sure you'll want to hear all of this, but I dug up some things about him. And Lenora."

"She was a criminal informant," Clayton supplied.

"And a criminal," Lenora added.

An unknowing one, from what Clayton had heard so far. A man she'd loved had dragged her into a situation that could have put her in grave danger. But yeah, that still made her a former criminal.

Harlan hesitated again. "Remember Corey Dayton?"

Even with his memory problems, that was one name

Clayton would never forget. "He's the guy who shot me in the diner."

"Yeah," Harlan verified. "Like Lenora, Dayton was once a criminal informant. There's no official record of it, but my friend says he used some info that Dayton provided during an investigation."

Clayton looked at Lenora to see if she knew that, but she obviously hadn't. She shook her head.

"There's more," Harlan said, and there was a lot of concern in his voice. "According to my agent friend, when Dayton worked as a CI, he reported to none other than Special Agent James Britt."

Chapter Eight

Lenora forced herself to eat, though the way her stomach was churning, she wasn't sure she could keep it down. Still, she did it for the baby's sake. And for Clayton's. She was tired of seeing the worry in his eyes.

Worry that she'd put there.

Worry that was now mirrored in his brothers' eyes, too.

There were three of them at the dinner table— Harlan, Wyatt and the youngest, Declan. Stella, the family friend, was there as well, and even Clayton's foster father, Kirby. The man was in a wheelchair and looked every bit as sick as Clayton had said he was—salt-white hair, and his veiny skin seemed paper thin. He wasn't eating but instead had an IV bag hooked up to his arm.

An odd gathering indeed.

There seemed to be lots of silent communication going on, as if they were all wired into each other's thoughts. Except for her, of course. While all of Clayton's family seemed sympathetic to the danger she and the baby were in, she figured there was a massive amount of suspicion, too. Probably because of her criminal past.

"You okay?" Clayton asked her.

Lenora realized she was staring at the plate of lasagna again, so she took another bite and nodded. "It's my first time eating with four lawmen." She wanted to keep the conversation light since the mood was anything but. "I keep waiting for one of you to read me my rights and arrest me."

Her attempted humor didn't work that well. The corner of Clayton's mouth lifted. Stella's, too. But the remaining trio of marshals and their foster father didn't crack a smile, and the quiet tension returned.

They had plenty to discuss, but no one was discussing it. Maybe because they were all so familiar with what was going on. Or maybe the lack of discussion was to spare her feelings. It wasn't working, but then discussing the investigation wouldn't help in that department, either.

All afternoon Clayton had tried—and failed—to get more info on James's association with the dead man who'd shot Clayton. Ditto for more info on Quentin. He was a suspect now, along with James, and either one of them could be working for Riggs. However, Clayton had been able to find out that James was in serious debt from two failed marriages and child-support payments. Maybe the debt had made him desperate enough to turn to Riggs for cash and murder for hire.

"Heard you got a clean bill of health from the doctor," Stella commented.

It took Lenora a moment to realize the woman was talking to her. She nodded. Dr. Cheryl Landry had given Lenora a checkup and said all was well. A huge relief. Despite all the craziness going on, her baby was still her first priority.

"If you don't mind me asking," Stella continued, "how long have Clayton and you been together?"

Lenora nearly choked on the bite of lasagna she'd

just taken. She looked at Clayton, trying to figure out what or what not to say.

"We're not actually together," Clayton answered.

"The baby wasn't planned," Lenora added.

"But he or she is still very much wanted," Clayton added, as well.

That caused the others to glance around. If there'd been a picture of awkward in the dictionary, this would have been it.

"A grandbaby," Kirby said, his voice a weak whisper. "Always wanted one of those."

Stella nodded. "Well, if you'd asked me which of Kirby's boys would be the first to be a daddy, I wouldn't have said Clayton or Slade. Wyatt, for sure."

Wyatt didn't say a thing.

Clayton scraped his fork over the cheesy top of the lasagna but didn't eat it. In fact, he was eating less than Lenora was. "You don't think I'm father material?" he asked Stella.

"Didn't say that. I think you'll make a fine one, but before Kirby brought you here to the ranch, none of you boys exactly had good role models for daddies."

Lenora remembered the discussion with the Ranger investigating Webb's murder. And there were also the notes she'd read about Clayton's childhood. It'd been miserable. But then, so had hers.

"I didn't know my dad," Lenora said without thinking. It definitely wasn't something she volunteered often, but somehow it seemed less awkward than discussing her own pregnancy or Clayton's qualifications as a father. "My parents never married, and my mom never even told me my dad's name until after he'd died."

Clayton looked at her from the corner of his eye. Frowned and mumbled, "I'm sorry."

Yes. So was she, and unfortunately her mother's actions had affected Lenora's own. Sometimes for the good. Others, not so much. She'd gone through life needing her father, and she had learned his identity too late.

"I'm hiring a surrogate," Wyatt said out of the blue.

It was suddenly so quiet, Lenora could hear her own heart beating. Judging from everyone's expression, this was unexpected news. But at least the attention was off her for the time being.

"Before Ann died, we'd planned on having kids," Wyatt went on. His gaze swung to Lenora's. "Ann was my wife, and she passed away years ago from a rare blood disorder."

"I'm sorry." And she was. She didn't know Wyatt well, but she could see the pain still in his eyes.

"I've always wanted a kid," Wyatt added. Not defensively. He had a smoothness about him. Not just in his voice but his expression. "I figured I might never find another woman like Ann. In fact, I've decided I want to quit looking, so I'm hiring a surrogate."

"You think the timing is wise?" Harlan asked. "We're all pretty much suspects as an accessory to Jonah Webb's murder. And unless his wife comes out of a coma and clears our names, we're likely to stay suspects."

With everything else going on, Lenora hadn't given that investigation much thought, but it was clearly a dark cloud hanging over all of them.

"The Rangers could be investigating Webb's death for years," Wyatt argued. "After that, it could be something else. The job, the ranch, you name it. I figure there's no perfect time to be a father, and I don't want to put my life on hold." He paused. "Besides, next week would have been Ann's thirty-second birthday, and that's when we'd planned to start our family."

Stella made a sound of agreement, but that was the only response for several moments.

"How many embryos did Ann and you store before her treatments started?" Kirby asked.

Now Wyatt looked uncomfortable. "Only one was viable."

Lenora guessed that one viable embryo might not be enough to assure a pregnancy. She felt for Wyatt, but her level of discomfort went up a notch for another reason. This was a family discussion about a private matter, and she shouldn't be part of it. Still, it didn't seem right to just stand up and excuse herself.

"So there's to be two kids. Yours and Clayton's," Harlan grumbled. He was opposite of the smooth Wyatt. His voice was a rusty growl, and his sheer size made him intimidating.

"He's just worried he'll have to change diapers," Stella joked and gave Harlan's beefy arm a playful jab with her finger. Her expression turned more serious when she looked back at Wyatt, then Clayton. "News like this is good for the family and for you. Isn't that right, Kirby?"

Kirby made a sound that could possibly have been agreement. Everyone's attention came back to Clayton and Lenora again. Maybe because everyone was waiting for them to verify they would indeed be a family.

Something she couldn't verify at all.

Thankfully, the sound of the footsteps gave her a reprieve. But when she saw that it was another marshal brother, Dallas, Lenora wasn't sure it was much a reprieve this time.

"Sorry to interrupt your dinner." Dallas dropped the

folder on the table next to Clayton. "Agent James Britt
had it delivered to the office. It's the file on Quentin
Hewitt, and I thought you'd want to see it right away."

"I do." Clayton pushed his plate aside to make room
so he could open the folder.

"Agent Britt's still not returning my calls, though,"
Dallas added, looking at Clayton. "Did you manage to
get in touch with him?"

"No." And Clayton clearly wasn't pleased about that.
Neither was she. Because they wanted answers about
James's association with the dead hit man. "I've gone
over his head and called his boss. Maybe that'll get some
kind of reaction."

It would. But Lenora prayed it was a reaction that
didn't lead to another attack.

Lenora pushed away her plate, too, and moved closer
to Clayton so she could see what was inside the folder.
Hopefully no more surprises. She'd already had enough
of those for one day.

The first thing in the folder was a report saying that
Quentin had disappeared from WITSEC five months
earlier and included accounts of the three sightings of
him since then. One of those sightings had been on a
gas-station security camera in San Antonio. Another
at a bank in Austin, where he'd accessed a safe deposit
box. Probably where he had some cash stashed.

The third sighting, however, put her heart in her
throat.

Oh, mercy.

Two days before Clayton was shot at the diner, Quentin had been spotted outside her house in Eagle Pass.
Clayton lifted the report and underneath were copies
of photos.

Definitely Quentin.

And he was skulking around her house. Specifically, outside her back door.

"Who took these photos?" Lenora immediately asked, and she picked them up to have a better look.

Clayton put his attention on the rest of the report. "Says here that the task force had you under surveillance. *For your safety.*" His tone was skeptical, and for a good reason. The leader of the task force, James, was one of their other suspects. "And an agent took the pictures."

She wanted to curse. "I guess it didn't occur to James to tell me that someone from my past, a man who might want to harm me, was hanging around my house in the dark."

And maybe even doing the break-ins.

Someone certainly had. And they hadn't just hung around. The person had broken in, destroyed an expensive antique panel and vandalized the place.

Why hadn't this been reported to the cops who were investigating the break-ins? But Lenora didn't need anyone to answer that.

She knew.

If James or anyone else on the task force had reported it, then it would have blown Quentin's identity in WIT-SEC. Of course, Quentin had already skipped out of WITSEC by then, but maybe James hadn't reported it because he would have had to explain her association with Quentin. That might be classified.

But still…

Lenora got up from the table. "I need to talk to James. And Quentin."

Clayton was already shaking his head when he turned to her, and he stood, as well. "Too dangerous."

"Not if I take precautions." She had to tamp down the

frustration just so she could speak. How dare James do this to her and not even have the guts to tell her when he was face-to-face with her.

None of the lawmen or even Stella looked as if they were willing to help her contact the men. That wouldn't stop her.

"Do you even know how to get in touch with Quentin?" Clayton asked.

"Not directly, but maybe I can still reach him. Before he went into WITSEC, when he still thought we were on the same side, Quentin said if I ever needed to get in touch with him, I should send him an email. He apparently set up the account just for the two of us to use, and he gave me the password."

"And did you ever use it?" Clayton wanted to know.

"No," she quickly answered. "Never had a reason to communicate with him." Her gaze snapped back to the photo of him on her porch. "Until now."

Clayton huffed. "How would emailing him help?"

"An email might not tell me anything, but talking to him would." She waited a moment until the groans died down. "I could try to make contact with him and then give him the number of a prepaid cell that he couldn't trace."

Yet more groans, grumbles and plenty of raised eyebrows.

"I've known Quentin for years, and I think I can tell if he's lying when I ask him if he wants me dead. If he's not behind this, then James probably is."

"We have a secure laptop so she can send the email," Harlan offered. "A burner, too," he added, using the slang term for a prepaid phone.

Clayton shook his head, apparently ready to nix it, but Dallas spoke first. "It might take us days or longer to find Quentin so we can question him. This might be the fastest way to get answers. And it doesn't put Lenora or you in danger."

It was a good argument, but Clayton still didn't jump to agree. When he finally cursed, she knew he'd just conceded.

Harlan left the dining room, and a few minutes later he came back with both a phone and a laptop. He turned on the cell, booted up the laptop and went to a secure server. She put in the email address that included the name of his company plus her birth year.

Her hands were shaking when she wrote: "Are you there, Q? Call me. We need to talk."

She typed in the cell number, hit Send and then held her breath. If the message bounced, then it meant Quentin hadn't kept the account active. After all this time, that was a distinct possibility.

But it didn't bounce.

That didn't mean it wouldn't eventually. It also didn't mean Quentin would answer right away, or at all, but this was the first step to try to reach him.

"It could take hours for him to respond," Clayton reminded her. "Why don't you finish your dinner and then get some rest? I can monitor the computer and the phone. You're in the guest room just across from my room, so I can come and get you if he calls or emails."

She wanted to refuse, since she hated putting this unpleasant duty on Clayton's shoulders, but the truth was, she was exhausted.

"But you need rest, too," she pointed out. She knew for a fact he'd been battling that headache since the attack at the church.

"I can rest," he assured her. "The computer will beep if a message comes in."

Good. It meant he could sleep. Well, maybe. After everything they'd been through today, sleep wasn't going to be a sure thing.

"Thank you," she told him, and Lenora finished her glass of milk. Like the lasagna, she didn't want it, but she couldn't neglect her health.

"If Quentin calls you back," Stella said, "maybe Clayton can put the fear of God into him. A badge can do that to some men. Especially men with plenty to hide."

"A lead bullet makes a stronger impression than a tin badge," Kirby mumbled.

It seemed an odd thing for a former lawman to say, but Lenora had to agree with him on this. If Quentin was out to kill Clayton and her, then she would do anything to stop him. There was no way she wanted Clayton taking a life and risking death for her again.

They said good-night to the others, and Clayton put the burner phone in his pocket and the laptop under his arm before they made their way up the stairs.

"Tomorrow I'll need to arrange to talk with Riggs," Clayton said on the walk to the guest room.

It wasn't exactly a surprise. She knew Riggs would have to be interviewed, but she dreaded Clayton having any contact with Jill's killer. But Lenora wanted to hear what Riggs, like Quentin, had to say about this latest shooting.

"I won't go to the prison, though," Clayton continued. "I'll try to set up a computer interview here at the ranch. That way you'll be able to watch."

"Thank you." And she was thankful that they might get some answers, but more than anything she just wanted it to be over because it felt as if someone were picking at all of her old wounds.

Clayton opened the guest-room door and turned on the light for her. Earlier, he'd shown her the room so she knew where it was in the maze of upstairs rooms, but she was surprised and thankful to see the clothes and toiletries lying on the king-size bed. The items hadn't been there before, and with everything else going on, it had slipped her mind that she had nothing else to wear.

"Dallas's fiancée, Joelle, sent over the clothes," Clayton explained. "Not sure if they'll fit, but maybe you can make do." And his gaze skimmed over her body.

"Yes," she mumbled, sliding her hand over her belly. "I'm not exactly thin these days."

"It suits you." His gaze moved to her eyes now, and the comment seemed a little more than just a reassurance. It had a trace of the heat they'd been battling all day.

Actually, ever since they'd met.

Clayton cleared his throat. "The Sadler's Falls sheriff is arranging for someone to get your things from the hotel where you were staying. And your car." He paused. "That doesn't mean I want you trying to leave. If you don't want to stay here for your sake, then I want you to think of the baby."

Since she had been thinking about leaving, that hit a nerve. "Being here puts you in danger," she reminded him.

"Your leaving would put me in even more," he quickly answered. "Because I'd go looking for you. All my brothers would, too, and it'd tie up resources that we should be using to find the person behind the bullets."

She frowned. Because it made sense.

"We have over a dozen ranch hands," he added. "Plus, the house has a security system wired to every window and door. I can't swear you'll be one hundred percent safe here, but I can say that I'll do anything to protect the baby and you."

And that's what she feared, that she would get Clayton shot again. Still, she wouldn't refuse his offer of protection. For now, anyway.

She nodded and expected her tentative agreement would spur a good-night from him. But he didn't move. He did give her another of those heated looks again, then mumbled something she didn't catch.

"Yes," she agreed. "This is a distraction we don't need." She didn't clarify *this,* because Lenora was certain he knew what it meant.

"I'm trying to remember why it wouldn't be a good idea to kiss you."

That robbed her of her breath and a good chunk of her common sense. "Because we have other things we should be doing."

"We're waiting," he pointed out, tipping his head to the laptop.

True. But there were other reasons. Ones that took a moment to recall. "You don't even remember being with me."

"My body does."

Oh, mercy. It was a bad reminder, and Lenora forced herself to remember there would be consequences for something as simple as a kiss.

"There's the baby." Her voice was whispery now. "You're still dealing with the notion of parenthood with a practical stranger. It's probably best to work that out before we add anything else to the mix."

"Yeah," he agreed. And he even added a nod. But that wasn't agreement in his eyes.

Clayton reached out, slid his hand around the back of her neck and pulled her to him. His mouth was on hers before the little sound of surprise could make it past Lenora's throat.

The pleasure was instant and so were the memories of their other kisses that had landed them in bed. That should have been a big red-flag warning to Lenora. She should have just pulled away.

But she didn't.

She kissed him right back.

Kissing him was like sipping expensive whiskey. And lots of it. She felt drunk and completely aroused after just a few seconds.

He wasn't exactly gentle. There was an urgency in the kiss that raced through her like wildfire. He deepened it, reminding her of his taste and also reminding her that he was very good at this.

Without breaking the kiss or the hold he had on her neck, Clayton eased the laptop onto the dresser, hooked his arm around her waist and brought her even closer to him. His body against hers.

Oh, yes. More memories that she didn't need.

Did that stop her? No. Lenora took everything she shouldn't be taking and allowed the heat to slide over every part of her.

It didn't take long for the urgency and hunger to get stronger, and while he took her mouth as if he owned it, they began to grapple for position. Trying to get closer to each other. Not exactly possible with her baby bump, but soon it seemed as if every part of her was touching every part of him.

Well, almost.

There was a part of her burning for a touch of a different kind, and she had very vivid memories of that, too. Clayton wasn't just a good kisser. He had carried that *good* directly into bed.

And if she didn't stop, that's exactly where they'd land now.

Lenora forced herself to move away from him. Not easy to do. That unsatisfied part of her let her know it wasn't pleased with her decision. But it was the right thing to do, and she was certain when her body cooled down that she would remember why it was right.

Maybe.

"Did it bring back any memories?" she asked, trying once again to keep things light. Hard to stay light, though, with her breath gusting, and she was sure her face was flushed with arousal.

He was pulling in hard breaths, too. "Not yet. Maybe we should experiment one more time." And then he smiled.

Her stomach did a flip-flop, because that smile was a powerful weapon in his manly arsenal. She wondered how many women that smile and those kisses had seduced.

But she really didn't want to know anything about his previous lovers, so she pushed that uneasy thought aside. It became even more uneasy, because it shouldn't have made her uneasy in the first place.

Good grief.

She was falling for him.

Hadn't her experience with men taught her anything? She sucked at relationships, and if the danger didn't tear them apart first, she'd find some way to mess it up. She always did. She had literally failed at every relationship she'd ever had. That couldn't happen this time. She needed to stay on good terms with her baby's father.

But not too good.

Definitely no more landing in bed.

She'd have a much better shot at just maintaining a

friendship. If her body would only cooperate. And if she could get past those blasted memories of them in bed the night of Jill's murder.

"We should get some rest," she managed to say.

He studied her as if he might challenge that, but he finally nodded and reached for the laptop. Before he could pick it up, however, she heard the buzzing sound. Not from the laptop, but from the burner cell he'd shoved into his pocket. There was only one person who'd be calling on that phone.

Quentin.

"Are you up for this?" Clayton asked.

She nodded, and he handed her the phone. Lenora pressed the answer button, put the call on speaker and waited for Quentin to say something.

"Lynnie?" the man asked.

It was Quentin all right, and it was her real name. Lynnie Martin. But she'd stopped using it not long after she began working for the task force. Somehow, though, Quentin had learned about her Lenora Whitaker alias, because he'd found her house. The photo in his file had proven that.

"How are you? Where are you?" Quentin asked.

"I've been better." And she didn't intend to answer the second part of his question. "Someone's trying to kill me, and I wondered if it was you."

"God, no." There was no hesitation, and he sounded surprised. *Sounded.* "What happened?"

"Someone shot at me," she settled for saying. After all, this was a fishing expedition, and she didn't want to give him too many details. Just enough to possibly hang himself.

Quentin cursed. "Are you all right?"

"No. And I want to know why you were at my house in Eagle Pass."

"I wasn't…" But then he stopped. "Okay, I was. I was checking on you, or rather trying to do that. I'd read about Jill's shooting, and I was worried. How did you know I was there?"

"A friend told me," she lied. "How'd you find me?"

"Through an old contact."

And with that vague answer, the conversation ground to a halt. She looked at Clayton to see if he was buying Quentin's innocent act, but he obviously wasn't. He was glaring at the phone as if he wanted to jump through it and beat Quentin senseless. If he was guilty, Lenora wanted to do the same thing.

"My old contact also told me you were pregnant," Quentin finally continued. "Who's the father?"

She sucked in her breath. Mercy. Lenora hadn't wanted Quentin to know about the baby. Especially since he could be insanely jealous. Or at least he had been when they were together. At the time she'd thought that only showed how much he loved her, but in hindsight, it only showed that he could be possessive and abusive.

Hardly love.

"The father is someone I'd rather not discuss," Lenora answered.

"It's that marshal from Maverick Springs, isn't it?"

A chill went over her, because it wasn't just what Quentin said, but how he said it. He sounded past being just jealous, and she knew from experience that jealous men often did dangerous things. And Quentin was a criminal. Heaven only knew just how far he would go.

"I've been trying to find out how you've been,"

Quentin continued. "And other things. Like your location, for instance. I want to see you."

"Why?" Clayton mouthed, and Lenora repeated it aloud to Quentin.

"Why?" Quentin mimicked. "Because I'm in love with you, that's why. Because we were torn apart because someone ratted on me and forced me to work with the justice department."

Even though he hadn't said she was the one to rat him out, he probably knew it. He seemed to know everything else about her. But thankfully, not her whereabouts.

"It's too dangerous for me to see you," she explained. "Someone wants me dead, and until I find out who that is, I'm staying in hiding."

"Agent James Britt," Quentin tossed out there. "I'm betting you can trace the danger right back to him. He's a dirty agent, Lynnie."

"You have proof of that?" She wasn't disagreeing with him, and she definitely didn't like James's association with the man who'd shot Clayton.

"Not yet, but that's why we have to meet," Quentin insisted. "We have to figure out a way to bring him down. When and where can you meet me?"

Clayton shook his head again, probably to make sure she didn't agree to anything Quentin wanted. "I'll have to get back to you on that," she said.

Quentin cursed again. "I can tell a put-off when I hear it, and you're making a big mistake."

That sounded like a threat, and Clayton's glare heated up.

"You have no idea who you're dealing with," Quentin went on. "You've got a dirty agent on your trail, and you're trusting a man you shouldn't trust."

Lenora definitely didn't like the sound of that. "What do you mean?"

"Marshal Clayton Caldwell," Quentin spat out like profanity.

She looked at Clayton to see if he knew what this was all about, but he only shook his head. "What about him?" Lenora asked.

"He's trouble. The worst kind of trouble that can get you killed the hard way." Quentin punctuated that with more profanity. "Lynnie, you weren't the target of the shooting at the diner in Maverick Springs. Clayton Caldwell was."

And with that, Quentin hung up.

Chapter Nine

Lynnie, you weren't the target of the shooting at the diner in Maverick Springs. Clayton Caldwell was.

Quentin's words repeated through Clayton's head, and even though he wanted to dismiss it as the ranting of a jealous man, it wouldn't be wise to do that.

Because it could be true.

With the triggerman dead and no proof of who'd hired him, Clayton could have indeed been the target. And worse, it might not even be connected to Lenora or Jill's murder. He'd been a marshal long enough to make plenty of enemies who would want to see him dead.

But how could Quentin be so sure that triggerman had been gunning for him and not Lenora? Or for both of them?

Clayton silently cursed. He was tired of not having answers. And he was especially tired of seeing that worried look on Lenora's face.

She had that look now while she was watching him set up the computer in the office for the interview with Riggs. Even though she wouldn't be in the same room with Riggs, just seeing him would no doubt trigger nightmarish memories of Jill's murder.

Bad for her.

Maybe good for Clayton, though.

Because it might jog his memory, too. A lot of that night was still a blur. Bits and pieces of things. He remembered seeing the gun in Riggs's hand, the shot fired and Jill collapsing on the ground. Broken pieces, but pieces that he could still mesh together. But then the memories stopped.

Riggs's lawyer would use those memory gaps to try to discredit his testimony, and while it wouldn't be needed to convict Riggs of murder, his legal team might continue to chip away at the evidence and witnesses. All it took was a little reasonable doubt, and the jury might not convict Riggs of murder.

Yeah, getting his memory back was critical.

Not just for the trial, either.

He looked at Lenora's stomach. In just a few months she'd give birth, and while he would love the child no matter what, he wanted to remember the sex that had resulted in the pregnancy. It was one gap he didn't want to live with for the rest of his life.

"What is it?" he heard Lenora ask.

And Clayton realized he was staring at her. Not just her stomach, either. Her body. He got a split-second image of her naked and in bed with him.

But maybe that was wishful thinking. After all, he was attracted to her, so it wasn't much of a stretch to picture her as his lover.

"Nothing," he said.

Her left eyebrow lifted a fraction, but she didn't have time to press him for a real answer, because at that moment, there was a beeping sound to indicate that Riggs was in place at the prison for the interview.

Clayton had already taken some precautions by making sure there'd be nothing on the screen that Riggs could use to identify their location. The dark curtains were drawn, and he'd positioned the desk so that the only background visible was a now-bare wall. Of course, that didn't mean Riggs wouldn't guess where they were, but Clayton didn't want to give the killer any kind of confirmation of that.

"Ready?" he asked Lenora.

She nodded, and more concern went through her eyes, but she faced the screen head-on. So did Clayton, and he pressed the button.

Riggs's face instantly came into view.

"Marshal Caldwell," Riggs greeted, flashing a smile. He was wearing a bright orange jumpsuit and his slumped-forward posture indicated that he was cuffed at the ankles and wrists. "And Lenora's here, too. To what do I owe the pleasure of this interrogation?"

"It's not an interrogation," Clayton corrected. Not officially, anyway, since Clayton wasn't the investigating officer in charge of Riggs's case. "We just want to ask you a few questions."

Riggs wasn't alone. There were two men in suits, one on each side of him. His lawyers, no doubt. Clayton had figured they'd be there, but he hoped their presence wouldn't discourage Riggs from talking. Of course, even if Riggs *did* talk, he might not tell them anything.

"Questions?" Riggs repeated. He made a show of looking surprised by that. "Guess you'd want to figure out what's going on. Heard you and Lenora had a bit of trouble. You two are regular bullet magnets, aren't you?"

Clayton tried not to have any outward reaction to that, but he hated this man making light of an attack that could have killed Lenora, him and their baby.

"Did you have anything to do with these latest bullets?" Clayton asked.

"Certainly not." Riggs's tone was mocking, and a

smile tugged at the corner of his mouth. "You're mistaken again. Just like you were about the other incident involving that pretty little thing, Jill Lang. I didn't have anything to do with that, either."

"Other than killing her," Lenora mumbled.

Riggs made a tsk-tsk sound. "That's all speculation at this point. That's why we have trials in this country."

Clayton had to admire the man's audacity, but it was that same audacity and cockiness that would make it harder to get info from him. All he needed was for Riggs to slip up and say something they could use. Clayton didn't have anything specific he could use to unhinge the man, but he was ready to bluff and make Riggs think that he did.

"You have a powerful motive for wanting Lenora and me out of the way," Clayton tossed out there.

Riggs shrugged. "I'm sure you have a lot of confidence in your skills on the witness stand, Marshal, but I have that same confidence in my lawyers. So there goes any motive you might think I have to silence you."

It was pure bravado. There was too much evidence against him, but Clayton didn't want to get into the specifics of the trial.

"If you didn't hire someone to fire those bullets at us," Clayton said, "then who did?"

"Oh, so now you want me to do your job for you?" Riggs taunted.

"No. But if you didn't have anything to do with it, you might want to use this opportunity to clear your name. Well, clear your name about this, anyway."

Clayton braced himself for another smart-mouth reply, and to help motivate Riggs, he added, "We've been studying your prison visit logs and communications we have authorization to view from your lawyers.

Not just their communications with you, but with others. It seems as if everything we uncover about this attack leads directly back to you."

One of the lawyers, a bald guy with a shiny head and face, immediately leaned over and whispered something to Riggs. The other lawyer, who was much younger, nodded. Which meant they'd likely told their client not to comment.

But Riggs spoke anyway. "I hope that doesn't mean you've done something illegal, like wiretaps or peeking at privileged lawyer-client communications."

Now Clayton shrugged. "The justice department's involved." And that was a reminder that the JD could indeed get wiretap approvals. They hadn't in this case, not that Clayton knew of, anyway. But it was a threatening reminder that secrets often didn't stay secrets for long.

"Agent James Britt is investigating," Clayton added.

More whispers from the lawyer, but Riggs pushed him away with his forearm and nailed his gaze to Lenora and Clayton. "You're both fools to trust Agent Britt." He practically spat out the man's name. "Yeah, he's investigating the shooting, but it's only to save his own hide."

Clayton didn't like the way James's name kept coming up in conversations that linked him to what was going on with them.

"What does that mean—he's trying to save his own hide?" Lenora pressed.

Again, Riggs pushed aside his lawyer's attempt to say something to him. "I mean if you want to check some *communications,* take a long look at Agent Britt's." Riggs paused, smiled again. "He's connected to the shooter at the diner."

That felt like a punch to the gut. Clayton already

knew about that connection, that Dayton was a criminal informant, but he'd only recently found out.

How long had Riggs known?

And how had he found out? Judging from Riggs's smirk, he wouldn't volunteer that, but Clayton tried anyway.

"What do you know about James and the dead hit man?" Clayton pressed.

"Only what I've heard through the grapevine. A lot of talk goes on here in prison. Talk about you, for instance." Riggs was looking at Lenora now. "Talk that you're a lot more than you claim to be." He leaned closer to the screen. "Ever worry that your involvement with Agent Britt could have caused your friend Jill to die?"

Lenora didn't react. Well, no facial reaction anyway, but Clayton saw the slight tremble in her hands. Yeah, this was the bad-memory part.

"I don't know what you mean," Lenora answered.

"Sure you do, sweet cakes. But if you want to keep your secret life a secret, that's fine with me. I suspect the marshal already knows it all anyway." Riggs paused, got that smirky look again. "But what Marshal Caldwell might not know is how all of this points right back to *him.*"

"Great," Clayton mumbled. He met Riggs eye to eye. "More word games. Why don't you just come out and say what you're skirting around?"

"All right." And Riggs's smile returned. "If you want to know who's behind these plots to kill you, you should look in your own backyard."

Clayton cursed before he could stop himself. Lenora reached out, took his hand. She shook her head. Obviously she thought he was about to lose it, but Clayton was in control.

Mostly, anyway.

Maybe it was yesterday's visit from the Ranger or the whole mess with Webb's murder, but he was just sick and tired of hearing allegations like that.

"You'd better not be implicating my foster father or brothers," Clayton said through clenched teeth.

"Wouldn't dream of it." Riggs leaned closer to the screen again. "I meant you should look in your own DNA backyard."

Clayton didn't have to choke back any profanity that time, because his throat snapped shut. He reminded himself that Riggs was a killer and a liar, and he would say anything to get Clayton to snap, for the pure pleasure of it.

"Oh," Riggs said. Butter wouldn't melt in his mouth. "I see you didn't know. Finally, I have news that even the marshals haven't been able to uncover."

"What news?" Lenora snapped, and she gripped Clayton's hand tighter.

Riggs made them wait while he gloated for what seemed an eternity. "That Melvin Larson, Clayton's father, is, well, a person of interest in your investigation. At least, he should be."

Lenora's gaze flew to Clayton's. Clearly she wanted an explanation, but he couldn't give her one. He had no idea why Riggs had just mentioned his worthless father.

"What does Melvin have to do with this?" Clayton demanded.

But Riggs was already standing. "This interview is over." And with his lawyers on each side of him, Riggs disappeared from view.

Hell.

It was an answer all right, but it wasn't an answer Clayton wanted.

"Why did Riggs say that about your father?" Lenora asked.

Clayton nodded but didn't add more, because another face appeared on the screen. It was the prison worker who'd set up the interview with Riggs.

"Get what you needed?" the worker asked.

Not even close, but Clayton mumbled a "thanks" and cut the feed.

Lenora quickly got to her feet. "Riggs is probably lying about your father's involvement."

"Birth father," Clayton automatically corrected. Melvin Larson wasn't much more than a sperm donor in Clayton's eyes. "And he doesn't even deserve to be called that. My mother and he never married, so I use her maiden name."

She paused, studied him. Paused some more. "Is Riggs lying?"

Clayton had to shake his head. "I don't know, but I intend to find out."

He reached for his phone so he could get some calls started, but Lenora stopped him. "Maybe Riggs said that to get us off track. I mean, it won't be easy for you to confront your birth father. Riggs could be doing this to distract us so we won't focus on the real culprit—him."

Clayton couldn't discount that, but he had to check out the lead Riggs had just given him, and that meant he had to face down the bastard who'd abandoned him at Rocky Creek when he was just a kid. Part of him welcomed it, because he was no longer a scared kid, but the other part of him worried that Lenora was right.

That this was some kind of setup or distraction orchestrated by Riggs.

Before Clayton could start the arrangements for a *chat* with Melvin, the house phone buzzed, and he saw on the screen that the call was from the senior ranch hand, Cutter Flores. Since Cutter rarely called the house, Clayton snatched up the phone.

"A problem?" Clayton immediately asked, and he put the call on speaker so Lenora could hear.

"I'm thinking yeah, it's a problem all right," Cutter replied, his voice and tone crusty.

Clayton groaned. "What happened?"

"I'm holding a Colt forty-five on a fella who just rode up on a Harley. We're out here at the end of the road on the cattle guard, and he says he's gotta see you and Miss Lenora right away. I messed up and let it slip that you were both here."

Great. Just what they didn't need. He didn't want anyone knowing Lenora was there. Of course, that cat was already out of the bag with James, and heck, even Riggs might have suspected her location.

"Who is he?" Clayton hoped like hell it wasn't Melvin. He wasn't ready for him and needed to do a current background check.

"Says his name is Quentin Hewitt," Cutter answered.

Lenora pulled in her breath. "Quentin's here at the ranch?"

But it wasn't Cutter who answered.

"I can stop Lynnie from being killed," another voice said. Quentin's, no doubt. "So tell your ranch hand to step aside before someone gets hurt. Because I'm not leaving until I talk to both of you."

Chapter Ten

Lenora dropped back down into the chair and shook her head. This was not a complication that Clayton and she needed, especially after the draining conversation they'd just had with Riggs. Of course, there was no good time for her to chat with Quentin.

"Lynnie?" Quentin called out from the other end of the phone line. "I know you're there, and we have to talk *now*. I wouldn't have come all the way out here if it wasn't important."

She didn't doubt that, but what was important to Quentin might not be safe for Clayton and her. After all, he was a suspect in the attacks.

Well, he was a suspect thanks to another suspect—James.

Both were men from a past that she hoped wasn't coming back to haunt her. If so, it would also haunt Clayton, and maybe even his family, in the worst possible way.

"How did you know I was here?" she asked Quentin.

"Wasn't much of a stretch to figure out that you'd come here to *him*."

The *him* said it all. It was a mix of anger, jealousy and other emotions that she didn't want to identify. Dealing

Send For
2 FREE BOOKS
Today!

I accept your offer!

Please send me two
free Harlequin Intrigue®
novels and two mystery
gifts (gifts worth about $10).
I understand that these books
are completely free—even
the shipping and handling will
be paid—and I am under no
obligation to purchase anything, ever,
as explained on the back of this card.

❏ I prefer the regular-print edition
182/382 HDL FVYQ

❏ I prefer the larger-print edition
199/399 HDL FVYQ

Please Print

FIRST NAME

LAST NAME

ADDRESS

APT.#   CITY

STATE/PROV.   ZIP/POSTAL CODE

Visit us online at
www.ReaderService.com

with Quentin under the best of circumstances could feel like trying to cool the fuse of a lit powder keg.

"She didn't come to me," Clayton fired back. "I found her about thirty minutes before a pair of gunmen did. Now I'm wondering if you set up that attack and if you're stupid enough to try another one here at the ranch."

Quentin didn't answer right away, but Lenora could practically feel his anger soaring. "I wouldn't hurt Lynnie. Not ever. And besides, you have your cowboy goon holding a gun on me, so there's zero chance of me living up to your delusions and hurting her."

"And I'll keep holdin' it on him," Cutter said, "until I hear different from you, Clayton."

Clayton certainly didn't tell his ranch hand to put down the gun, which was smart. Because despite Quentin's claim of not wanting to hurt Lenora, she had no idea what he had in mind. That gun was a layer of security that she didn't want to remove.

"What's so important that you have to tell me?" Lenora pressed.

"If you want to find out, you'll have to see me." Quentin's voice wasn't as smug as Riggs's, but it was close.

Both Clayton and she groaned, and he held his hand over the phone so that Quentin wouldn't be able to hear them. "You think he actually has something important?" Clayton asked.

She had to shake her head again. "It's possible, but it's just as possible that he's using this to see me."

Clayton's mouth tightened. "Quentin's still in love with you?"

"He was never in love with me." That had become obvious once the relationship had gone on for a while.

"More like an obsession. He likes to own and control things. Humans included. For some reason, he especially enjoyed controlling me."

She saw the question in Clayton's eyes and didn't make him ask it. "And I was never in love with him. I thought I was. But it didn't take long for me to discover that he wasn't the man he was pretending to be."

That was likely a reminder for Clayton that she'd been guilty of the same thing. Pretending to be in need of protection when she'd been a deep-cover agent. The irony was that she had indeed needed his protection.

Still did.

But she was afraid protection would come at a huge cost. Losing her heart to him, for one thing. And she was certain neither of them was ready for that. Not with this investigation and Clayton's coming to terms with the baby he'd never planned to have.

"You want to see him?" Clayton asked her.

"I want to question him," she clarified. "And I want to know if he has anything we can use to figure out who's trying to kill us."

Clayton stayed quiet a moment before he moved his hand from the phone. "Cutter, are you alone with our visitor?"

"Nope. Got Deke and Ray here, too."

"Good," Clayton mumbled. "Make sure he's not armed and then take him to the hay barn. We'll talk with him there." He ended the call, looked at her. "I don't want him in the house, and I don't want to be hanging around outside while we talk."

Oh, mercy. It hit her then. Quentin might not have come alone. After all, the two gunmen from the church attack hadn't been found yet, and they could be working for Quentin. He could have brought them here, all under the guise of trying to help her.

Lenora gave a frustrated groan. She wasn't stupid, so why was her head so foggy? She wanted to blame it on the stress, but she had to stop thinking like that. Because it could get her killed.

Clayton unsnapped the leather strap on his waist holster so that his weapon would be easier to draw. "You're sure you want to do this?"

She nodded. "I think I have to do it."

He didn't argue with that. He hitched his head toward the door, and she followed him out of the ranch office and into the hall, then down the stairs and toward the door that led to the covered back porch.

It was a cloudy day, thank goodness. Maybe that would cut down Clayton's chances of getting a migraine. He didn't even put on his sunglasses, but he did look around. No doubt for any signs of the gunmen. However, everything looked normal.

Lenora soon realized why Clayton had chosen the hay barn. It was just a short walk from the back of the house, and in under a minute he had her inside the massive structure. Both the end doors were open, letting in a breeze. Still, it was hot.

"Here are the rules," he said, looking at her. "You stay behind me, and you don't take any chances."

She nodded again and intended to do just as he'd asked. "I just want answers and then for him to leave."

"Yeah," he mumbled, and glanced down at her stomach. Then her mouth. "I think I'm remembering the night we were together."

Oh.

Well, she hadn't expected that, and for some reason it seemed a little, well, embarrassing. Like talking about sex after the fact, and in this case, long after. Months, to be exact.

"What do you remember?" she asked.

"Just a flash of an image here and there." He reached out, lightly raked his thumb over her chin.

"Naked images?" She winced a little. Definitely a question she should have kept to herself.

"Some, yeah," he verified. He groaned and stepped back. "It didn't exactly make for a restful night's sleep."

Lenora made a sound of agreement. She'd had a lot of nights like that since she'd met Clayton, and another one the night previous night in the guest room. It hadn't made it easier for her to know that he was right across the hall.

His gaze came back to her again. No pain this time in all those dark brown swirls of his eyes. "What made you come to my bed that night? Was it just the pain over losing your friend?"

The question threw her for a moment. She opened her mouth to say yes, but then she rethought that. It was the pain that had sent her to his room, but she hadn't been so blinded by grief that she couldn't have said no to him.

"It's complicated," she settled for saying.

"It always is." The corner of his mouth lifted just a fraction before he leaned in and touched his lips to hers.

The touch barely qualified as a kiss, but it was a jolting reminder that she shouldn't just be melting into a relationship with him.

Clayton's forehead bunched up. Obviously he'd noted the concern on her face, but he didn't have time to ask her about it. The sound of the approaching vehicle caught their attention, and Clayton moved in front of her as soon as the three men stepped from the truck and walked into the barn.

A man who appeared to be in his late fifties came in first. He wore jeans and a battered cowboy hat. Cutter, no doubt. And he looked as crusty and weathered as he'd sounded on the phone.

Quentin came in next, but it took Lenora a moment to recognize him. She'd never seen him wear anything but one of his pricey suits in public, but he, too, was wearing jeans and boots. Maybe because he'd ridden in on a Harley—yet something else unfamiliar about him. He'd always preferred top-of-the-line sports cars.

The third man who walked into the barn behind Quentin was younger, early twenties, and judging from the way he was dressed, he was probably also a ranch hand. However, like Cutter, he was armed with a Colt.

"I had Deke stay down by the gate," Cutter explained. "Just in case this fella here had a friend or two follow him."

That helped steady Lenora's nerves a little. Until she remembered that hired guns might not use the road. They might try to sneak onto the ranch while Quentin kept them occupied. Clayton must have been thinking the same thing, because he leaned in and assured her, "The other ranch hands are keeping watch."

"No need for it. I didn't bring anyone with me," Quentin insisted.

He stepped around Cutter and likely would have made a beeline for her, but Clayton put his hand over his gun and moved slightly forward. That brought Quentin to a grinding halt, but he still didn't look at Clayton. Instead, her ex pinned his attention to her. Or at least what he could see of her from over Clayton's shoulder.

"Lynnie." Quentin said her name on a rise of breath. Almost as if he was relieved to find her actually there.

But the relief or whatever it was quickly faded, and his eyes narrowed. "I know," he said.

Lenora had to shake her head. Was he talking about the baby? If so, he'd already made it clear that he wasn't pleased that she was pregnant with another man's child. But she immediately rethought that. The one thing she was certain of was that Quentin hadn't loved her, that he'd only used her in his illegal business practices. So maybe he didn't care whose baby she was carrying.

"You know what, exactly?" Clayton asked for her.

Quentin stabbed his index finger in her direction. "Plenty of things. For one, I know you were working undercover to investigate me."

Her heart felt as if it dropped to the barn floor. That info was classified. Of course, some people knew— Clayton and James, for instance. But James had assured her that Quentin would never be privy to that.

Because Quentin could be dangerous.

After all, she'd conducted a secret investigation into his illegal business affairs that had ultimately led to his arrest. True, he hadn't gone to jail, but it had forced him to cooperate with the authorities.

"Don't bother to deny it," Quentin went on. "I don't want to hear another lie come out of your mouth. You worked for the justice department. Sneaking around my company and handing over private files to Agent James Britt. You had no right to do that."

Lenora knew she should just stay quiet, but that riled her to the core. How dare he put all the blame on her? "I turned over files because you're a criminal. You were laundering money for drug cartels and anyone else who could make you some fast cash."

Clayton gave her a warning glance, probably to remind her to say quiet, but she ignored him. "How did you find out about this?" she demanded.

"Well, obviously not through you, that's for sure." Quentin cursed, but his expression actually softened a bit. "Lynnie..." And that's all he said for several moments. "Could we go somewhere private and talk?"

"No," Clayton said before Quentin got out the last word of his request.

Quentin's eyes narrowed again. "Why don't you let Lynnie speak for herself?"

"You'll get the same answer from me," she quickly replied. "I don't trust you, Quentin. You've been stalking me. You broke into my house—"

"Not stalking. I was looking for something you stole from me."

Clayton looked back at her to see if she knew what he was talking about, but she had to shake her head. "Everything I took from your office, I handed over to Agent Britt," she insisted.

"Not everything. There were files on an offshore oil rig account."

Lenora had to dig through the memories of her search, and she remembered plenty of other accounts, but nothing to do with offshore oil.

"Don't pretend you don't know," Quentin snapped. "It's stupid and dangerous to keep those files. People would kill for them."

His anger was so strong she could practically feel it, and even though he didn't come closer, suddenly his presence felt a lot more menacing than it had just seconds earlier.

"What people?" Clayton demanded.

"Criminals you don't want to deal with." He cursed, and it took Quentin a while to regain his composure.

"These men are bad, and Lynnie's playing with fire by holding on to files they want."

Fed up with not being able to face him head-on, Lenora stepped out from behind Clayton. "I'm not holding on to anything. I washed my hands of you when I found out you'd involved me in your criminal activities. In fact, I believe you could be the person who's trying to kill us."

Quentin's attention dropped to her stomach. He didn't seem surprised with the baby bump, but he did look disgusted when his gaze volleyed between her and Clayton. Quentin's next round of profanity was especially bad. He huffed and put his hands on his hips.

"Oh, I get it now," Quentin said. "I thought you came to the marshal because you believed he could protect you. But it's more than that. You're in love with him."

"No. We're not in love. We're not even together like you think," she answered, because it was true and she didn't want Quentin aiming his jealous venom at Clayton.

But she quickly realized it was too late for that. And now Clayton was looking at her, silently asking if she'd forgotten all about that kiss.

She hadn't.

Not a chance of that.

But letting Quentin see that she did have feelings for Clayton would be like poking a rattlesnake with a stick.

"I don't want you dead," Quentin finally answered. But his cold, hard look let them know that feeling didn't extend to Clayton.

"You said on the phone that you believe I was the target of the shooting at the diner," Clayton reminded him. His voice was all business now, and like her, he probably just wanted this visit over and done. "Why do you think that?"

Quentin hesitated so long that Lenora wasn't sure he'd answer. "I don't think it. I *know* it."

She looked up at Clayton, to give him a silent reminder that anything coming out of Quentin's mouth could be a lie, but his gaze was locked to Quentin's.

"You got any proof or even an explanation to go with that?" Clayton demanded.

"I've got *information*." And Quentin's expression changed again. Not for the good, either. It seemed as if he was gloating or something. "You want the proof, find it yourself, Marshal."

"I'll do that," Clayton assured him, "but first I'll need this so-called information."

"It's not so-called. It's real. Riggs has teamed up again with someone he used to work with a couple of years back. This guy doesn't have the cash or the brains to orchestrate an attack like the one at the diner, but I figure Riggs provided both in ample amounts."

Yes, Riggs could indeed do that. With his money and resources, all he had to do was find someone he could pay enough to do his bidding. Or someone he could manipulate. Of course, that person could be the man standing directly in front of them—Quentin.

"Riggs hired a former business associate?" Lenora asked. And yes, she was very skeptical of this info. "If it's true, why doesn't the justice department know about this?"

But she had to concede that maybe they did. James could have withheld it from her, especially if he was a dirty agent working for Riggs. He could also be withholding those files that Quentin had just mentioned. *If* they existed.

Was James that former business associate?

Or was this another lie that Quentin was trying to use to muddy the waters?

That gloating look in Quentin's eyes went up a notch. "Because the justice department has criminal informants, but I have informants who are still criminals. On active duty, you could say. And no, I'm not naming names. These are people who'll kill you for betraying them."

She didn't doubt that part, but there was still a key piece of information missing here.

"You got a name for Riggs's business partner?" Clayton pressed.

No glare this time. Just more of that gloating, self-satisfied look. "Lynnie's met him a time or two because back in the day I used to hire him when I needed some muscle."

Lenora had to shake her head. "I have no idea what you're talking about. Not just the *muscle,* either. I didn't know you'd ever hired any muscle. And as for anyone specific, I met dozens of people when I worked for you. Even more afterward, when I was working for James to bring you down."

Quentin didn't seem to have a reaction to that last jabbing reminder. "But you remember this guy. He came in a couple of times while you were still working for me. Or rather, pretending to work for me. A guy in his fifties, always wore a white cowboy hat with one side kicked up. He went out to dinner with us once."

That was enough to jog her memory. Lenora did indeed remember a man like that, but she hadn't known he was hired muscle. However, that wasn't what bothered her now. It was that gleam in Quentin's eyes.

Something about this wasn't right on many levels.

She forced herself to think, to try to recall any details she could about the man. Lenora picked through the conversations she'd heard between Quentin and the man in the white hat.

And her heart nearly skipped a beat.

"Oh, God," she said, and her gaze flew to Clayton. "I didn't know. I swear, I didn't know."

Clayton looked at her as if she'd slugged him. "Didn't know what?"

Lenora had to explain. She had to make him understand. "I only met him a time or two, and I didn't make the association until just now."

Quentin smiled. "What Lynnie is stumbling around trying to tell you is that the man she and I worked with was none other than Melvin Larson. Your dear ol' dad."

Chapter Eleven

The anger slammed like a fist into Clayton's chest, and after seeing the look on Lenora's face, he knew that Quentin wasn't lying. Not about this, anyway.

"Get him out of here," Clayton told Cutter and the other ranch hand, Ray. "And make sure he's off the ranch and doesn't come back."

Clayton caught one last glimpse of Quentin's smile. A smile he wanted to dissolve to dust, but he forced himself to remember that Quentin was just the messenger. Yeah, he could still be guilty all the way up to his eyeballs, but he wasn't lying now.

He waited until Cutter and Ray had the man out of his sight, and Clayton yanked out his phone so he could call Harlan at the marshals' office.

"I don't want to answer a lot of questions about what I'm about to ask you to do," Clayton said the moment his brother answered. "But I need you to find my birth father right away and bring him in for questioning."

"All right," Harlan said without hesitation. "And if he resists?"

"I hope to hell he does," Clayton mumbled, and he ended the call.

"Let's go," Clayton said to Lenora. But he didn't just say it. He snapped it and got them moving.

"I'm sorry," Lenora repeated.

Clayton wanted to assure her that he didn't blame her for what'd just happened, but his throat clamped shut, and he couldn't speak. It didn't help that the sun broke through the clouds at that exact moment and the pain stabbed through his head.

"Come on," Lenora insisted, and she reversed the grip and took hold of him. "Let's get inside."

He did. They hurried across the narrow strip of yard and driveway and back into the house. Thankfully no one was in the kitchen or other rooms that they went through, because Clayton didn't want to explain what he was still having trouble dealing with.

Melvin might have been behind these attacks.

The SOB could have killed not just him, but Lenora and the baby.

With Lenora right behind him, he stormed up the stairs to the ranch office where he'd had the earlier computer interview with Riggs. At the time, Clayton had thought that was enough hard news to swallow, but here he'd been given another jolt.

"I honestly didn't remember your father until Quentin said those things," Lenora told him. Her voice was frantic now, and she moved in front of him to force eye contact.

Every nerve in his body felt raw, and the emotion was at a rolling boil inside him. It didn't help that Lenora looked as if she was ready for him to toss her out the door. Clayton was ready to do something, but he wasn't sure what.

Before he could think—which should have been a big red flag that anything he was about to do would likely be a mistake—he moved toward her. And he made that mistake anyway. He latched on to Lenora, dragged her against him and kissed her.

With the rage burning him, he forced himself to stay gentle. Not just with his mouth, but with his embrace. He tried to hold her as if she were fine glass that might shatter under too much pressure. Still, despite his holding back and the battering of emotions, he felt something else.

The sheer pleasure of her taste.

It soothed him. The sweet coil of heat that rippled through his body. The way she felt in his arms. Her scent. And that little purr that she made deep within her throat. All of it helped.

Then hurt.

Because the need twisted, and while he could feel the anger softening and melting away, the rest of him was far from soft. Obviously a certain part of him thought he was about to get lucky, but that couldn't happen.

At least he was pretty sure it couldn't.

Clayton turned, and without breaking the hold they had on each other, he shut the door and pressed Lenora against the back of it. If he was going to be stupid, he didn't want someone walking in on them.

The kiss got hotter and deeper, and they couldn't seem to get close enough to each other. Was this how it'd been the night they had sex? This overwhelming urge to do whatever it took to ease the pressure building inside them?

And this was a *them* situation. Because Lenora darn sure wasn't a passive participant.

She worked her hands down his back, pulling him closer and closer. The new angle gave him perfect access to her neck, so Clayton lowered his head and dropped some kisses there.

Lenora made another of those sounds.

That revved his body into full gear, and he caught onto the back of her leg, adjusting the angle again so that her sex was against his.

Clayton nearly dragged her to the floor.

Man, he couldn't take her like this. Okay, he could. But it might not be safe. He'd never had sex with a pregnant woman, and while that only seemed to add to this furnace of heat he was battling, he didn't want to take any risks and hurt her.

Using every bit of willpower that he could muster, he caught on to her shoulders and moved her back just a little. Just enough so that the intimate contact was gone.

"I'm sorry," he managed to say. "I shouldn't have taken my bad mood out on you."

"Give me a second to catch my breath and cool off." She looked up at him, blinked. "That was a bad-mood reaction? Remind me to get you in a bad mood more often." She gave a nervous laugh and waved him off. "Forget I said that."

He'd have an easier time forgetting that he had an erection.

Part of him was pleased that she could make light of this. The other part of him wasn't. He needed a big reason to stay away from her, and just telling himself that she was off-limits wasn't doing the job.

With her chest still pumping for air, she reached out and ran her hand down his arm. It wasn't foreplay. Probably meant to comfort him. And much to Clayton's surprise, it did.

"I don't blame you for not remembering my birth father," he said right off the bat. "I don't think for one minute you intentionally withheld that info."

And maybe that made him stupid. Because while Lenora and he were in danger together, that didn't mean they were together.

"For what it's worth, I didn't deal directly with Melvin." She paused. "I take it he's a crook or he wouldn't have had an association with Quentin."

"Oh, yeah. He's a crook, all right. Never committed a federal offense—not one that I could find, anyway. If I had, I would have gone after him."

Another pause. Another touch on his arm. "Would Melvin really want you dead?" she asked.

"If the price was right, he would. And I figure Riggs would pay a great deal of money to get us out of the picture."

Lenora made a sound of agreement and slid her hand over her stomach. "And he wouldn't give a second thought to the baby." She huffed. Groaned. Moved away from him. "I thought if I left that it would be safer for you. I made plans to leave," she added, snagging his gaze.

"You what?"

She didn't exactly look pleased about having to tell him this. Good. Because Clayton wasn't pleased to hear it.

"I made some calls last night on the burner cell so they couldn't be traced," she explained. "I managed to make arrangements for a place in Dallas. I figured leaving was the best way to keep you alive."

There it was. Yet something else she'd withheld from him. "Did you plan on telling me, or would you have just left the way you did the day I was shot?"

Her silence let him know the answer to that. "I trust you, but I thought I'd be doing you a favor."

He tried not to be angry with her. He succeeded at that, but not at nullifying the frustration.

Clayton walked to her and looked her directly in the eyes. "You can't leave. I know it's not fair because you're the one who has to go through this pregnancy, but that's my baby, and I want to be part of his or her life. That includes keeping the baby, and you, safe."

She certainly didn't jump to agree with him. "But at what cost? You could be killed."

"Any cost," he let her know. And it wasn't lip service. He hadn't planned on fatherhood, but Clayton realized the baby was one of the most important things in his life.

Family.

"After we find who's trying to kill us, we'll sit down and work out, well, whatever we need to work out."

She stared at him, probably ready to ask if that whatever included sex. Yeah, it likely would. Despite not needing the distraction, Clayton couldn't see a way around it. Their bodies just lit up like firecrackers when they were around each other, and since he didn't intend to let her out of his sight for long, that meant a lot of heat.

His phone buzzed, and he saw Harlan's name on the screen. "Well?" Clayton greeted his brother, and he hoped it was good news for a change.

"I made some calls and found the SOB. Melvin's at his new place of business in San Antonio. He's selling souvenir imports from Mexico."

Yeah, finding him was good news, all right. Maybe it would get even better. "Please tell me Melvin's business is a front for drugs or something else illegal?"

"SAPD will check it out," Harlan verified. "Are you up for an interrogation?"

"With Melvin?" Clayton clarified.

"Yep. I have a friend over there at SAPD, Lt. Nate Ryland, and he's offered to bring the father of the year here to Maverick Springs."

Clayton's stomach tightened. He wanted to see Melvin, but he dreaded it, too. "How soon?"

"Soon," Harlan said. "Lt. Ryland is picking him up now. They'll be here in about two hours."

Not long of a wait, and not much time to plan what to do with Lenora. Despite his earlier thought of not letting her out of his sight for long, he might have to do just that to keep her safe.

With help from one of his brothers, that was.

Clayton ended the call and turned to her. "I want you to stay here while I go into town."

The head shaking started almost immediately. "I want to see Melvin and hear what he has to say."

"Too risky. Best if you stay here. I'll call Dallas and have him come out and stay with Stella, Kirby and you while I talk to Melvin. I won't be long, promise."

He saw the moment that Lenora surrendered to that idea, but she also wasn't pleased. Still, he preferred her riled to being in danger. Or in the same room with Melvin. Which might be the same thing.

His phone buzzed again, and for a moment Clayton thought it was Harlan calling with something he'd forgotten to say. But it was Cutter again.

"Please tell me Quentin didn't give you any trouble leaving the ranch," Clayton said when he answered.

"No, he left, all right. But we got another kind of trouble."

Before Clayton could groan or ask what that trouble was, he heard something he didn't want to hear.

A gunshot.

THE SOUND OF THE SHOT stopped Lenora cold. She'd been on the verge of asking Clayton who or what had put that troubled look back on his face, but that shot was the answer to her question.

God.

What had gone wrong now?

Clayton pulled her to the floor even though she'd already started in that direction anyway, and he drew his gun from his holster. She'd left her weapon in the guest room, and Lenora cursed her decision to do that. The ranch had felt safe.

Judging from that shot, that was a false sense of security. Now she had no immediate way to defend herself.

If that was indeed what she would have to do.

Lenora held out hope that one of the ranch hands had fired at a snake or something.

"Where?" Clayton demanded. Lenora knew it was Cutter on the other end of the line, but she couldn't make out what the man was saying.

Another shot cracked through the air, and Clayton jabbed the end-call button and scrambled to the window so he could look out the corner of the blinds.

"Stay down," he told her.

That and his suddenly vigilant stance let her know this wasn't someone shooting at snakes. *No.* It could be Quentin or those two gunmen who'd tried to kill them at the church. Either way, they were under fire.

"Stella?" Clayton called out.

"Was that a gunshot?" the woman immediately asked.

"Yes." And Lenora could tell that it hurt for him to say that. "Get Kirby on the floor and away from the windows."

Hopefully Stella would do as he said, but even with

the nurse's help, it wouldn't be easy for the two women to get a sick, weak man to a safe place.

The third shot blasted into something. The barn, maybe. Judging from the sound, their attacker was using a high-powered rifle, which meant he wouldn't have to be too close to deliver those shots.

"Who's doing this?" she asked.

"Not sure." Clayton moved to the other side of the window and winced when he looked out. No doubt because of the light in his eyes.

Lenora wanted to suggest they trade places. She was a good shot and the light wasn't a factor for her, but there was no way Clayton was going to let her do that.

When his phone buzzed again, Clayton slid it across the floor toward her. "Answer it and put it on speaker."

Lenora did, and she extended her hand so the cell would be closer to him. "What's going on out there?" Clayton immediately asked. "Can you see the shooter?"

"Not anymore," Cutter explained. "I got just that one glimpse of him by the back pasture fence, and he disappeared into the trees."

And was probably in one of them by now. On their short walk to the barn to talk to Quentin, Lenora had noticed plenty of towering oaks just on the other side of that fence, and in parts it was thick woods. About a quarter of a mile from the house.

Easy range for someone armed with a scope rifle.

"I called the others," Cutter added. "They're on the way."

Yes, but they were coming from town, which meant they were at least twenty minutes out. Plus, they couldn't just come driving onto the property and risk being shot. They'd have to work out some kind of plan for a safe, indirect approach, and that would take precious time.

There was another shot, but this time Lenora didn't have to guess what it hit. Not the barn. This one had gone into the back of the house.

"Kirby's room is back there." Clayton's breath was gusting now, and he must have realized he wouldn't get a look at the gunman from this particular window, because he scurried away from it and to the door.

"Come on," Clayton finally said. "Stay low and behind me. I need to get to the back of the house so I can try to pinpoint this gunman."

"You have an extra weapon?" she asked.

"I don't want you shooting. I don't want you anywhere near the line of fire." But even after issuing that warning, he rifled through the bottom desk drawer and came up with another semiautomatic.

The moment the gun was in her hand, Clayton got them moving. Thankfully, the stairs were at the front of the house, away from those bullets that continued to come at them.

The timing of the shots was odd. Spaced out five to six seconds. Hardly a barrage, but maybe the gunman hoped to get a lucky shot by firing randomly into the house. He could also be saving ammo. That didn't put her at ease any, because it meant he could prolong the attack.

There was a powder room just off the entry, and Clayton threw open the door and got her inside. Probably because it had a limestone floor and no exterior walls or windows. It was no doubt one of the safest places in the house. Unlike Kirby's room. Even though she hadn't been inside it, she knew it was on the back corner of the building.

Right where the gunman was firing.

"It shouldn't take my brothers long to get here," Clayton said, and he gave her what was probably meant to be a reassuring glance. It didn't work, because Lenora saw the concern all over his face.

Clayton didn't waste any time. He started running, and Lenora picked through the gunfire and the other noises in the house so she could listen to his footsteps. It didn't take long before she could no longer hear them, but she did hear Stella's frantic voice.

God, she hoped that Kirby hadn't been shot. Or worse. It sickened her enough to know that this monster was after Clayton and her, but she didn't want his foster father pulled into the middle of this.

More footsteps.

Clayton was probably moving them to a safer location. The footsteps weren't far away from her when Lenora heard and felt the loud blast.

Another shot.

But this one hadn't come from the back of the house. This bullet had torn through the front door. That sent her already-racing heart beating even faster. Because they weren't just dealing with one shooter, but with two.

At least.

Heaven knew how many of them were out there, waiting to kill them.

Clayton threw open the powder room door and practically pushed Kirby, Stella and the nurse inside. There wasn't a drop of color in Kirby's face, and the two women looked terrified. This couldn't be good for Kirby's already-fragile health, and she hoped it didn't cause a setback. Clayton was already dealing with enough guilt over these attacks, and he'd never forgive himself if Kirby got hurt.

It was a tight fit when all four of them piled into the small room, but since Lenora was the only one of them armed, she worked her way to the doorway so she could try to protect them if the gunmen got into the house. It wasn't something Clayton would want her to do, but they didn't have a choice.

Lenora nearly caught Clayton by the arm when he started toward the front door. Right where the second shooter had targeted. But the sound caused him to go to a standstill.

Sirens.

Lots of them.

His brothers were on the grounds, and while it didn't mean they were safe, she liked their odds better now they had some serious backup.

Just like that, the shots stopped. However, Clayton didn't. He hurried to the front door and looked out. Lenora couldn't see what immediately caught his attention, but she clearly heard his profanity.

"Stay put," Clayton warned all of them.

"You can't go out there," Lenora warned him right back.

"I can't let him get away."

Clayton spared her a glance from over his shoulder, and she saw the warning repeated in his expression. He didn't want her trying to help, and even though that was exactly what she wanted to do, Lenora had to concede that someone needed to stay inside with the others. At least until Clayton's brothers managed to make their way to the house.

Clayton barreled onto the porch, slamming the door behind him, and she heard him start running. She also heard something else.

A shot.

Probably not Clayton's, either, because this one sounded farther away from the house than he probably was. That meant someone could have shot at him. She couldn't quite choke back the fear that slammed through her.

Mercy, how had things come to this?

"Clayton's gonna get killed," Kirby mumbled. "Give me that gun so I can help."

The man could barely stand, so Lenora doubted he could get off a decent shot. But she could. "I've had training," she said to him. "And I've saved Clayton before."

Of course, it was possible she'd created the danger that required him to be saved in the diner, but that was guilt she'd have to deal with another time. For now, she needed to focus on the gunfight going on just on the other side of the front door.

Staying low, Lenora scrambled across the entry and levered herself up slightly so she could look out one of the sidelight windows. She wasn't sure what she would see, but she immediately spotted Clayton.

Just as he threw himself to the side of his truck.

It wasn't a second too soon, because a bullet slammed into the side of the vehicle.

That put her heart in her throat, and she'd never felt more helpless in her life.

The shooter darted out of the line of fire, too, and landed behind a tree. He was a white male, mid-thirties, wearing dark clothes. Lenora tried to commit everything about him to memory in case the guy got away.

He was armed with what appeared to be a Glock long-range pistol. Definitely not an amateur's weapon. She was almost positive he was one of the same men who'd attacked the church.

A dozen bad possibilities went through her mind, and she replayed both shootings, especially the one at the diner. More than anything she wanted to help Clayton, but she couldn't risk going out there. After all, there was a second gunman, and if he made his way into the house, Kirby, Stella and the nurse were sitting ducks.

So Lenora prayed. Waited. Watched.

Clayton levered himself up from the ground, and in the same motion, he took aim. So did the gunman, who moved out from the cover of the tree.

Both men fired.

She couldn't tell who got off a shot first, but Lenora soon saw the results. Their attacker crumpled into a heap on the ground.

Lenora didn't release the breath she'd been holding, didn't stop praying. Until Clayton got to his feet. He was all right, thank God. The gunman had missed him.

"The other one took off," Cutter shouted. "He's already hightailed it over the fence."

Clayton looked around and spotted Dallas and Wyatt hurrying on foot toward them. "Go after him," he instructed his brothers.

He didn't follow the two. Instead, Clayton ran to the fallen man and touched his fingers to his neck.

"We need to get him to the hospital now," she heard him tell Cutter. "I want to keep him alive so he can tell us why the hell this just happened."

Chapter Twelve

While he paced in the marshals' office, Clayton went through his mental checklist and made sure he'd done everything to keep everyone safe.

Well, as safe as he could.

Considering Kirby was refusing to leave the ranch, that meant even his best measures still weren't very safe. Clayton had tried and failed multiple times to convince his foster father to go to the hospital, so that meant formulating a backup plan.

Step one was to beef up security. Arm the ranch hands and have them keep watch to make sure another intruder didn't make it onto the grounds. He'd also need all the suspects questioned again. Information was the key to finding out who was behind these attacks.

The second part of the plan wasn't nearly as easy, because it involved finding the gunman who'd escaped. So far, there hadn't even been a sighting for them to follow. Still, they'd keep looking and might get lucky. Might get lucky, too, with the wounded gunman, who was still in surgery. If he made it out alive, and that was a big *if*, Clayton would be able to question him and maybe get answers about who was behind these attempts to kill Lenora and him.

"Are you sure you're okay?" Lenora asked him—again.

"Yeah," Clayton answered again.

Lenora had echoed the same response each of the times he'd put that particular question to her, and he was thinking it was a lie for both of them.

It was true—she hadn't been physically hurt—but the adrenaline and stress of being under fire couldn't be good for her or the baby. That was why he'd insisted she have a physical, and even though the doctor had given her the okay, it was on Clayton's mental list to figure out a way to make things better for her.

"You could delay this interview," Lenora reminded him.

He could, but it would just put off the inevitable. Clayton didn't especially want to see Melvin. He'd written the man out of his life a long time ago. Seeing him would no doubt bring back memories that no longer mattered in the grand scheme of things. But what Melvin's impending arrival had done was force Clayton to bring Lenora out into the open.

Despite all the beefed-up security, Clayton hadn't wanted to leave her at the ranch, even though Dallas had offered to keep an eye on her. He trusted Dallas with his life, but Dallas's hands were full, since Kirby, Stella, the nurse and the housekeeper were all there at the house.

And besides, Clayton wasn't sure that Lenora wouldn't try to run.

She had that look in her eyes—the fear that she was somehow putting him in even more danger by staying nearby. But Clayton figured this visit with Melvin could dispel that notion. Because if Melvin was the person behind the attacks, then Clayton himself, not Lenora, was the primary target.

He'd been careful on the drive from the ranch to the Marshals building, and had made sure they weren't followed, but that didn't mean she was safe even though they were surrounded by lawmen. Maybe she wasn't safe anywhere.

"Cheer up," his brother Declan said. "Maybe Melvin will resist coming in and the lieutenant will have to arrest him or something."

"Maybe," Clayton mumbled, though he didn't want that happening with Lenora around.

Declan was at his desk, working. Or rather, appearing to work while keeping watch for Melvin's arrival. Wyatt and Harlan were doing the same. Clayton, too, was at his desk trying to get through the mountain of paperwork that had been piling up in his absence, but it was hard to work with his mind flying in a dozen different directions.

"Showtime," Harlan announced. "Lt. Ryland just pulled into the parking lot."

And that meant the wait was finally over. For him, anyway. Clayton turned to Lenora, who was seated in the chair next to his desk.

"I know," she said before he could speak. "You don't want me to take any unnecessary chances."

"I don't even want you in the same room with him," Clayton insisted.

He didn't give her a chance to argue. Clayton led her to the observation room, where she'd be able to watch but Melvin wouldn't be able to see her. Clayton's boss, Saul Warner, was already in the interview room, working on some paperwork while he waited for Melvin to arrive. Clayton had offered to do the interview solo, but his boss had nixed that.

Probably a good thing, too.

Hard to be objective with a man he hated, and objectivity was something sorely needed in this investigation.

Thankfully, Clayton had found a few bits of info that Saul might be able to use in the interview. The problem was none of those bits in themselves would lead to Melvin's arrest. They needed a confession, and barring that, they needed more evidence. Still, this interview was a start.

"Afraid I'll punch Melvin if I get close enough to him?" Lenora joked.

Clayton appreciated her attempt to keep this light. Appreciated it even more when she idly brushed a kiss on his cheek. But then she froze and pulled back, as if she'd realized what she'd done. This wasn't a steamy kiss like the one in his office, but it was yet another reminder they were becoming too comfortable with each other.

If their situation had been different, that would be a good thing. But when Clayton looked at her now, all he needed to see and remember was the danger.

He shut the door and turned just as a dark-haired guy in a white shirt and jeans walked in with Melvin. Lt. Ryland, no doubt. Melvin wasn't cuffed, but the lieutenant had a firm grip on his arm. Ryland looked around the room and spotted Harlan, who took them toward the interview room.

"Look what the cat dragged in," Melvin said, his attention zooming straight to Clayton.

Clayton cursed the knot that tightened his stomach. Cursed even more the cobweb of images this man had left in his mind. He couldn't remember his night of sex with Lenora, but he could recall in complete detail that Melvin had made his life a living hell.

It'd been years since Clayton had seen him, and those

years had not been kind to him. He was still on the beefy side, but his hair was iron-gray now, and he had enough wrinkles that it was well past the stage of calling them character lines. Melvin Larson looked every bit of his fifty-six years and then some.

"He's all yours," the lieutenant said.

"Looks as if he *cooperated*," Clayton mumbled.

"Yeah," Ryland verified, and he sounded disappointed, too. Maybe Harlan had told him all about Clayton's prize of a father. "But I'll have to wash my car to get rid of the slime of snake oil he left behind. Hope you can take him down a notch or two. Better yet, arrest him for something. *Anything*."

Clayton managed a smile, thanked Lt. Ryland and went into the interview room.

"Melvin Larson," Saul greeted before Melvin had even taken a seat. "I'm Marshal Saul Warner, and you're about to answer some questions." Saul didn't leave any room for doubt about that. It certainly wasn't an invitation.

"I'd be glad to." Melvin didn't just sit. He lounged in the chair, stretching his legs out in front of him and tucking his hands behind the back of his neck.

Clayton blew out a long breath. He hadn't forgotten how cocky the man was, but that was a stark reminder. So was his sheer size. When he was a kid, Clayton had been on the receiving end of Melvin's fists, and even though that size didn't intimidate him now, he recalled Quentin's accusation—that Riggs had used Melvin as hired muscle. That was exactly the kind of job Clayton could imagine Melvin taking.

And enjoying.

"Always willing to lend a helping hand to the law," Melvin added.

Saul, clearly not impressed with Melvin's offer, gave him a flat look from over the top of his reading glasses. "I understand from Clayton here that you've been named as a person of interest in an attempted-murder investigation. Not just one attempt, either, but rather several of them."

"Me?" Melvin drew that out a few syllables. "Must be mistaken. I'm a respected businessman. I import piñatas, serapes, leather belts and the occasional piece of silver jewelry." He showed them his turquoise-and-coral-studded watch.

"I'll make sure SAPD checks those piñatas for drugs," Clayton said.

That caused some of Melvin's cockiness to dissolve. "Always was an ungrateful son."

"Always was a dirtbag of a father," Clayton fired back.

Melvin shrugged. "Probably because I never wanted to be one." He looked at Saul when he talked. "His cheap tramp of a mother ran out on us when he was five. Did my best to raise him right, but you know being saddled with a kid just wasn't my idea of a good life."

"But selling piñatas is." Saul didn't wait for an answer to that smart-mouthed comeback. "So, tell me, Mr. Larson, what's your association with Adam Riggs?"

"Former association," Melvin instantly corrected. If he was surprised by the question, he certainly didn't show it.

"Your association," Saul corrected right back, and he handed Melvin the paper that Clayton had given Saul earlier. "It took a little digging, but according to this, the money you used to open your business was funded through an offshore account owned by none other than Adam Riggs."

Now there was a reaction. Melvin shot Clayton a glare that could have chipped solid stone.

He glared back at Melvin. "So what's your association with Riggs?" Clayton repeated.

"He's a minor investor in my business, that's all." And he dismissed it with a wave of his hand.

Clayton and Saul both mumbled some profanity, because they weren't dismissing anything. "One more lie and I'm going to throw your sorry, lying butt in a jail cell," Saul warned him. "And to make things fun, I'll give Clayton the flippin' keys while I take a long dinner break."

Melvin's glare got worse. "All right." No more lounging. He sat up in the chair and pulled back his shoulders. "Riggs loaned me the entire amount for my import business, and in addition to the money I give him to repay the loan, he gets thirty percent of the net profits."

That meshed with what Clayton had learned. It was a pricey loan, because along with the thirty percent, Melvin was paying interest on the loan itself. Over half his profits were going to Riggs. Of course, a man with Melvin's history likely wouldn't have been able to get a conventional loan, so Riggs might have been his only option.

Clayton went closer, put his hands flat on the table and leaned in. A clear violation of Melvin's personal space. "So what kind of deal did you make with Riggs— that in exchange for killing me, he'd cancel your debts?"

"No." Melvin volleyed glances at both of them, and maybe for the first time he realized this was serious. "No," he repeated.

"Come on, are you saying you don't want me dead?" Clayton pressed, staring at the man.

Melvin didn't break the stare. "Well, I didn't think

so much about it until I came in here and you started accusing me of things I'm not doing. So yeah, maybe now I'm thinking about it, but I didn't do anything to make it happen."

"Does that mean you're not Riggs's hired hit man?" Saul pressed.

"That's exactly what I'm saying. I don't play hired gun for anybody. Riggs included. And I'm also thinking it's time for a lawyer. Hell's bells." Melvin added some much-worse profanity. "I didn't know I'd come in here and get accused of attempted murder."

Melvin seemed genuine enough about that, but Clayton didn't believe the man was innocent in all of this.

"I'm calling a lawyer," Melvin insisted and took out his phone.

Saul gave Clayton a look that he needed no words to interpret. This interview was over until Melvin's attorney arrived. However, before Melvin could make the call, Clayton heard voices in the hall, and he threw open the door to make sure something hadn't happened to Lenora.

She was there in the doorway of the observation room, but she wasn't alone. James was with her, and Harlan and Lt. Ryland were right behind the agent.

"What are you doing here?" Clayton asked James. He also stepped out so he could move in front of Lenora. He didn't think James was stupid enough to try to pull something in a marshals' office, but he wasn't willing to take that chance. However, James no longer had his attention on Lenora.

It was on Melvin.

"Is *he* a suspect in the shootings?" James immediately asked.

"He's a person of interest," Clayton clarified. That

was the official answer, but the truth was yeah, he was a suspect. "You know him?"

"I know of him." James spared him a glance. "He's your father."

Lenora groaned. "Please don't tell us he's a criminal informant, too."

"No. But he is someone that the task force investigated along with Riggs. We didn't find enough evidence to arrest him, and he wasn't trustworthy enough for us to use him in the sting operation that got us Riggs."

Clayton hadn't expected to be informed of any and all federal investigations, but it riled him that he hadn't been told of this one. Especially since Melvin could be a hired assassin.

Clayton studied the body language of both men. James had on his lawman's face. All business, all cop. But sweat popped out on Melvin's face.

"I'm leaving," Melvin announced. "You want to keep me here, arrest me. Then I can sue you for harassment."

Clayton glanced at his boss, but Saul only shook his head. "We investigate and build a case if there is one. Then we make the arrest." He turned back to Melvin. "Don't leave the state, because I'll be bringing your butt right back in here as soon as we have something," he added.

Clayton wished he could stop Melvin from storming out of the room, but the irony was, the law was on Melvin's side.

Melvin stopped right in front of James. "You'd better watch this one, Clayton."

"What does that mean?" James demanded before Clayton could ask first.

But Melvin only gave that laid-back smile. Except

this time, it didn't look so laid-back. Melvin was spooked or something.

"You need a ride?" Lt. Ryland asked Melvin.

Melvin shot them all dirty looks. "No, I'll find my own way back. I've had my fill of all of you badges."

James watched Melvin leave and mumbled something that Clayton didn't catch. "I'll send over anything we have on him," James offered. "It won't be much, though, and certainly not enough to make an arrest. Still, it might be useful."

Clayton thanked him, but that didn't ease the suspicions he had about James. After all, the agent had essentially stopped the interview just by showing up. He hadn't warned Melvin to stay quiet, but that's exactly what he'd accomplished.

"My advice?" James said, talking to Saul now. "You need to stop Clayton and Lenora from digging into this investigation. God knows who Riggs hired to do his dirty work, but this is no time to have an assassin's sights on Lenora."

"I believe his sights are already on me," Lenora reminded him.

"Then this is the time to lie low. If you won't do it for yourself, then think of your baby."

"We have been," Clayton assured him. And it riled him that James believed *he* was only thinking of Lenora and the baby. "But it seems as if we keep getting the runaround from you. You dole out info only after the fact."

Every muscle in James's face went stiff. His mouth tightened. "Are you accusing me of something?"

Clayton lifted his shoulder. "Yeah. I thought it was obvious."

"If you've got something to say, say it," James insisted.

Clayton obliged. "You're in debt up to your eyeballs from alimony and child support."

Clearly, that didn't please James. "My debts are none of your business."

"They are if those debts are putting us in danger," Lenora spoke up.

Clayton wasn't sure which one of them got the icier glare from James. "I'm not going to dignify that with an answer."

Which, of course, clarified nothing, and there was certainly no dignity in dodging a question that could lead them to the person who wanted them dead.

Lenora moved closer, looked James in the eyes. "Quentin seems to think you have some files from his former business associates. Files that might have something to do with these men who are out to kill us."

James made a sound of disgust. "And of course Quentin is telling the truth." He cursed. "The only files I have are the ones you gave me after your investigation, and there's nothing in them that could put your life at risk. The risk comes from Quentin." He tipped his head toward the door where Melvin had exited. "Or from that piece of work who just left."

"We're keeping an eye on both of them," Clayton quickly assured him. "But I consider you a person of interest, too. Just like my birth father and Quentin. I think any one of you could be working for Riggs."

James's glare became even more intense. "Prove it." And with that challenge, James walked out.

"You really think he's dirty?" Lt. Ryland asked.

"Hard to tell, but he's been keeping secrets." Like not telling them about his association with the hit man.

"Plus, it seemed to me that Melvin shut up awfully fast when he saw James."

Both Saul and Lenora made sounds of agreement.

"My brother's FBI," Ryland said. "I can have him make some calls and ask some questions."

Clayton wasn't about to refuse any help. "Thanks. I'd appreciate that."

The lieutenant left, and since Lenora already looked exhausted, Clayton made plans to do the same. There was just one problem with that.

Where to go?

The ranch hands were still repairing the bullet damage to the house. Besides, Lenora might not even be able to rest there with the god-awful memories of the attack.

"I need to make arrangements for a safe house," he let her know, and he scrubbed his hands over his face to give him time to catch his breath.

"You're making the ranch safe," she reminded him. "Plus, you know that's where you need to be, since Kirby won't leave and go elsewhere."

No, Kirby wasn't budging, but he couldn't let that be a reason for returning. "I have to put your safety first."

"And you can do that at the ranch." She huffed, probably because she realized she wasn't convincing him. "Look, I'm worried about bringing the danger to your family, but I don't think it'll go away just because we're not there."

She was right about that. No matter where they went, the gunmen would still likely come to the ranch looking for them. If only he could get Kirby to go somewhere with them. Of course, his foster father was known for his pigheadedness.

"Since Kirby's not giving us a choice, I'd rather be surrounded by marshals I trust. Including you," she added. "If I'm tucked away at a safe house, the worst could happen there. Another attack. Especially since Quentin and James don't seem to have any trouble finding us."

That was true. But he still wasn't convinced. "A safe house is still our best bet." He saw the argument in her eyes—that he couldn't make any place safe enough—but then he saw something else. "You're not thinking of running anymore."

Lenora blinked, obviously surprised that he'd picked up on that. "Not thinking of it in the near future," she corrected.

Well, that was a start, but it wasn't nearly good enough. Not with the stakes this high. "We need to make the time to talk."

She blinked, maybe troubled by that. Lenora and he always seemed to be on the same wavelength, so she probably sensed that the talk wouldn't just be about her safety. Nope. They had some personal stuff to work out.

That didn't include sex.

All right, maybe it did. But it included a whole lot more, and talking rather than sex was how they had to work things out between them.

Too bad his body was still trying to veto that idea.

"Talk," she repeated. "Something we can do at the ranch. Let's face it, Clayton. We don't have to reinvent a safety net at the ranch. There's one already in place. And besides, no lawman is going to give us as much backup as your family."

"You trust them?" he asked, because he was certain that Lenora wasn't exactly comfortable there.

"If you do, I do," she confirmed.

Well, he certainly trusted them all right, but that didn't mean this was the right choice.

On the other hand…

Maybe it was the bone-weary fatigue settling in or the realization that she was right—there was no safe place. But Clayton decided to go home, get some rest and hope that he could come up with a better solution for Lenora's safety.

He only made it a few steps before his phone buzzed again. With everything that had gone on, the first thing he thought of was Kirby, that maybe there'd been another attack at the ranch. But it was Dr. Cheryl Landry's name on the screen.

"Clayton?" the doctor said the moment he answered. "The guy you shot is finally out of surgery. We did the best we could, but he's in critical condition."

Not the best news he could have gotten, but at least the shooter was alive. That was a start.

"Can I talk to him?" Clayton asked.

"*If* he wakes up," the doctor clarified. "My advice is to come to the hospital and wait, because, Clayton, when and if he regains consciousness, he's not going to last long."

Chapter Thirteen

Lenora had never felt safer—and more vulnerable—in her entire life. She literally had three federal marshals guarding her as they went into the Maverick Springs hospital.

Clayton, Harlan and Declan.

However, with a hired killer still at large, she knew they could be attacked anywhere, anytime.

That included the hospital.

"We won't stay long," Clayton reminded her again while he led her inside the building.

He had his phone sandwiched between his shoulder and ear and was on hold. That didn't stop him from making some vigilant glances around the parking lot and the waiting room on the other side of the sliding glass doors. His brothers did the same.

"If this guy doesn't wake up soon," Clayton added, "we'll go back to the ranch and wait."

That, too, was a risk, because they might not make it back into town fast enough if he did regain consciousness and start talking. They could miss something vital, and all because they were trying to keep her safe.

Something she wasn't even sure was possible.

Clayton came to a quick halt in the waiting room, and for a moment Lenora thought he'd seen something or someone that might be a threat. But she soon realized he'd stopped because the FBI agent on the other end of the line, Kade Ryland, was giving him some information.

"We got a match on the wounded man's prints. His name is Peter Lomax," Clayton said the moment he ended the call, and he got them moving again, past the waiting room and down a wide corridor.

There weren't a lot of people in this part of the hospital, just medical staff in scrubs, but the marshals looked at each one of them as possible threats.

"Peter Lomax." Harlan tested the name as if deciding if it meant anything to him. He finally shook his head. "How long of a record does he have?"

"Long," Clayton verified. "In and out of jail since he was sixteen. He's worked for loan sharks and other lowlifes. But the good news is that he often works with his kid brother, Johnny. Agent Ryland's already put out an APB on the guy."

Good. They had a likely name for the second man who'd tried to kill them, and maybe the FBI or marshals could find him before he launched another attack. Of course, Riggs or whoever was behind this could just hire someone else.

Not a comforting thought.

It would take some doing, but if Riggs was indeed the culprit, they needed to find a way to cut off his funds so he couldn't do any more harm.

They hadn't made it to the surgical waiting area when Lenora spotted a familiar face coming up the hall toward them. Dr. Cheryl Landry.

"Any change in the patient?" Clayton asked. "Is he awake yet?"

"No to both questions. But come this way," the doctor said to them. "You can wait in my office."

It wasn't far, just a few doors down, and with her attention fully on Lenora, Dr. Landry ushered them inside, and then closed the door. "Right before the wounded guy was brought in, I got a call from Special Agent James Britt."

Clayton and his brothers mumbled, groaned and otherwise showed their disapproval about that.

"About me?" Lenora asked.

The doctor nodded and wearily dropped down into the chair behind her desk. "He was fishing to find out if I thought you were mentally competent or if you'd been brainwashed or something."

Clayton cursed. "Let me guess—he's trying to force Lenora into his protective custody, or something along those lines."

"Sure sounded like it to me," Dr. Landry verified, "but I told him Lenora was my patient and that I had no intentions of divulging anything about her."

"Thank you." Lenora eased into a chair, as well. She was relieved that the doctor hadn't told James anything, but she felt no relief that James had attempted to do something like this. Of course, if pressed, James would probably say he was just concerned about her.

And that might be the truth.

The problem was it was just too risky to trust him.

Clayton slid his hand around the back of her neck, rubbed gently. "James might not be the person out to get us, but there's no way I'd let him take you into protective custody."

She believed him, but Lenora hated that they had another distraction at a time when they were already dealing with too much.

"If he calls back," Dr. Landry said, "I'll transfer him to the hospital lawyer. That might get him to back off."

"Agent Britt could be the one who hired the guy you just operated on," Clayton warned Dr. Landry. "Be careful around him."

"I will." The doctor looked at the position of Clayton's hand and then Lenora's stomach. "If you want, I can arrange for you to have an ultrasound. For your own peace of mind," she quickly added, probably because she saw the alarm in Lenora's eyes.

Lenora nodded, thanked her again. With everything that'd happened, it might help if she could see her baby. The other checkup the doctor had given her hadn't included one.

"The nurse will call me if our guy wakes up." Dr. Landry went to the door, opened it and then froze. That's because someone was standing there.

Clayton automatically reached for his gun and stepped in front of Lenora. Harlan pulled the doctor behind him, and both he and Declan drew their weapons, as well.

Quentin was in the doorway.

The man laughed nervously and held up his hands in mock surrender. "Jumpy, aren't you?"

Lenora groaned at the joking tone and the fact he was there at all. "Nearly being killed will make anyone jumpy," she mumbled, and despite Clayton's attempts to stop it, she stepped out from behind him.

"What the heck are you doing here?" Lenora demanded.

Quentin lowered his hands, lifted his shoulder. "I just wanted to speak to you."

Clayton moved in front of her again. "Not going to

happen. The last time we spoke to you at the ranch, someone tried to gun us down."

"I didn't have anything to do with that," he huffed. "Look, there's no way I would hire someone to kill Lynnie. I want to save her."

"Not very convincing," Clayton fired back.

Since it was clear that Clayton wasn't going to let her face down Quentin, Lenora peered over his shoulder so she could make eye contact with him. She didn't want him to miss her glare.

"How'd you know I was here?" she snapped.

"I guessed." Quentin snapped, too, but some of the anger and tension melted away. "It's all over town about the man the marshal shot, and I figured he'd come here to check on the guy. Didn't figure he'd let you out of his sight."

"I'm not," Clayton verified. "And that's your cue to leave." He moved to shut the door, but Quentin blocked it with his foot.

"Move or you'll be sorry," Clayton said.

She didn't have to see his expression to know that every muscle in his face had turned to iron. She could hear it in his voice.

But Quentin didn't move. He reached in his pocket, causing all three marshals to train their guns on him.

"It's just a piece of paper," Quentin snarled. He stared at Clayton. "If you want proof of who's trying to kill you, call off your trigger-happy kin."

Clayton didn't say a word, and none of them lowered their guns. After several long moments, Quentin cursed, and using just two fingers he extracted a single sheet of paper from his pocket. Maybe because Harlan was the closest one to him, Quentin handed him the paper.

However, before Harlan could even read it, the doctor's phone beeped. She looked down at the screen.

"Our patient is awake," she said.

And that meant they had to wrap up this conversation—or whatever the heck it was—with Quentin.

"Are these numbers for some kind of account?" Harlan asked, and then he handed the paper to Clayton. Lenora looked as well, but they weren't familiar.

"One of Riggs's offshore accounts," Quentin supplied. "If you do a little digging, I think you'll see that Riggs had twenty-five thousand dollars transferred the day before those gunmen showed up at the church."

"How did you get this information?" Harlan asked at the same moment that Clayton asked, "Who received this money?"

"A friend of a friend told me about this," Quentin said, looking at Harlan first. Then he turned to Clayton. "I can't prove it, but my guess is your *daddy* was on the receiving end of the money. I haven't been able to get access to his accounts, but I'm thinking Melvin hid the cash he got from Riggs in his business. Wouldn't be hard to do."

Not with an import business, it wouldn't. All it'd take would be to falsify some orders. Like on silver watches.

"I'll start looking," Harlan volunteered, and he took the paper back from Clayton. "Should I take Mr. Helpful here into custody?"

"For what?" Quentin howled. "I'm trying to save your butts."

Clayton made a yeah-right sound. "Or maybe trying to help yourself by putting the blame on others. Report to the marshals' office for further questioning. Oh, and if you don't show up, there'll be an APB out for your arrest."

That caused Quentin to curse a blue streak.

"Hate to rush this," Dr. Landry said, "but this patient might not hang on much longer."

When the doctor started for the door, Quentin stepped back, probably because Harlan looked ready to knock him to the floor.

"You're welcome," Quentin snarled with his trademark sarcasm.

"I'll thank you if and when this pans out," Clayton let him know. He took Lenora by the arm and followed the doctor. Harlan and Declan were right behind them, and all of them, including the doctor, kept an eye on Quentin.

"He's dangerous, too?" Dr. Landry asked.

"Probably." Unlike Quentin's, Clayton's tone was apologetic. "I'll make sure security has photos of both Quentin and Agent Britt. And I'll arrange a guard for our shooter."

"The sheriff's already sent over a deputy," the doctor let him know. "You don't think that'll be enough?"

"Not in this situation," Clayton answered.

It hit Lenora then that the shooter was probably in just as much danger as Clayton and she were. After all, if his boss thought he was talking, or might talk to the marshals, then someone would try to eliminate him.

She glanced back at Quentin, who was still in the hall.

"Yeah," Clayton said, as if he knew what she was thinking. "If Quentin's still here when we finish talking with this guy, I'll have Harlan *escort* him to a holding cell at the headquarters."

Good. Lenora only wished they could hold Quentin indefinitely. Melvin and James, too. That way there'd be no more threat. Well, until Riggs hired someone else.

They wound their way through the maze of halls to the surgical ICU, and there was indeed a deputy outside one of the doors. He had a stocky build and round face. Maybe too young to face down anyone Riggs might send to silence the guy. Clayton was right to add more security.

"Marshals," the deputy greeted. According to his name tag he was Randy Wells, and he seemed to know Harlan, Declan and Clayton. Of course, since they were all lawmen, they had probably worked some cases together.

The deputy stepped aside so they could enter. She immediately spotted the man in the bed and knew this must be the person who'd tried to kill them, but he no longer seemed a formidable foe. His watery, weak eyes opened, and the moment his gaze landed on Clayton he wiggled his fingers, motioning for him to come closer.

Lenora wasn't sure she wanted Clayton closer to the man, but she doubted Peter Lomax was in any shape to launch another attack.

"I need a deal." Lomax's voice was a gravelly whisper, and each word was a struggle.

"What kind of deal?" Clayton asked.

"For my brother, Johnny." And that's all he said for several seconds. Lomax used that time to gather his breath. Or rather, try. He started to wheeze, prompting the doctor to check the machines.

"I have something that'll be useful to you," Lomax finally continued. "And I'll trade it for a lighter sentence for my brother."

"He took shots at us," Clayton reminded him.

"He was following my orders." Lomax pulled in a shallow, ragged breath. "And if you want to know whose orders I was following, then you gotta swear to give Johnny a break."

Clayton, Harlan and Declan exchanged glances. "All right," Clayton agreed, though Lenora had no idea if he truly would go through with it.

With his eyes barely open, Lomax studied him as if trying to decide if Clayton was telling the truth. Maybe he had his doubts, too, but if so, he didn't voice them. Of course, he didn't have a lot of options here. It was obvious that he was dying, and he might bargain with the devil to get what he wanted.

Lomax finally nodded. "It's in a wall safe at my sister's place up in Abilene." And with that, his eyelids fluttered back down again.

"What's in the safe?" Clayton asked when Lomax didn't continue.

"A recording." Lomax repeated his answer in a soundless mumble.

Clayton moved closer, until he was looming over the man. "What kind of recording?"

One of the machines made a shrill sound. "Everyone out now," Dr. Landry ordered.

"What recording?" Clayton pressed as they moved out of the room and back into the hall with Deputy Wells. "What recording?"

But Lomax didn't answer. In fact, he didn't draw another breath. A nurse pushed them aside and hurried into the room, shutting the door.

"I'll call the marshals in Abilene and get them started on a search warrant for his sister's place," Declan offered. He took out his phone, mumbled some profanity. "No signal in here." He glanced around as if he might consider leaving, but then shook his head. "It can wait a few minutes until we hear what the doc has to say."

Those few minutes passed slowly, and all of them kept watch just in case Quentin was still hanging around. No sign of him, though, and the doctor finally opened the door. One look at her face and Lenora knew that Lomax was gone.

Dr. Landry shook her head. "Honestly, I'm surprised he lasted as long as he did. I hope you got what you needed from him."

"Maybe." Clayton sounded cautiously hopeful.

Lenora knew how he felt. God only knew what was on the recording, but maybe it would indeed give them the name of the person who'd hired Lomax and his brother.

Clayton thanked Dr. Landry, and with Deputy Wells trailing along behind them, they started back down the hall. Still no sign of Quentin, but the moment they rounded the first corner, she saw someone else she didn't want to see.

James.

As he usually did, Clayton tried to step in front of her, but Lenora maneuvered around him so she could face James down. "If you're here to find out if I'm mentally competent, the answer's yes, and I want you to back off. I no longer work for you, and I won't have you meddling in my life."

All in all, it was a warning without teeth. There wasn't much she could do to get him to back off, but she was tired of staying silent while James tried to run roughshod over her.

"It's not meddling." James gave each of them a glance. "I'm here in an official capacity to question Peter Lomax."

"Too late," she told him. "He just died."

If James had a reaction to that, Lenora didn't see it. "Questioning him is just one reason I'm here."

Mercy. She didn't like the sound of that.

"You're not putting Lenora in protective custody," Clayton insisted.

"No." And judging from the way his mouth tightened, James didn't approve of it. "But the FBI is taking over this investigation. I plan to find Johnny Lomax and interrogate him until he breaks."

Harlan cursed. "Under whose authority? Johnny Lomax isn't a federal fugitive."

"Doesn't have to be if the local sheriff requests FBI assistance."

Clayton glanced back at the deputy, who only shrugged. "Sheriff Geary called in the FBI?" Clayton asked James.

"He did. And I'm the lead agent assigned to the investigation." James shoved his thumb against his own chest. "So, anything you learned from Peter Lomax, you're to tell me *now.*"

None of them volunteered a thing, not even Deputy Wells.

"Fine," James spat out. "Play all the games you want, but if you try to get any kind of search warrant or APB relevant to this case, I'll have all your badges."

With that warning, James pushed past them and headed up the hall, not in the direction of the exit, but straight toward Dr. Landry, who was outside the dead man's door.

"Let's go," Clayton said, hurrying them out of there. He looked back at the deputy. "You might not want to hear what I'm about to do. Wouldn't want you to get in trouble with Sheriff Geary."

The deputy confirmed that with a nod and got out of there fast.

"Should I call and get that search warrant?" Harlan asked.

Clayton shook his head. "I'll do it. I need to get that recording before the FBI does." Because if James got it first, he might try to destroy it.

He took out his phone and made the call.

Chapter Fourteen

The restless energy inside her made her want to scream, but Lenora knew there was nothing she could do but wait in the ranch office for some hopefully good news. In Clayton's case, along with the waiting, he was making calls and sending emails to try to speed things along.

It was a race against time, and Lenora prayed the Abilene police would get the search warrant for the recording before James got wind and stopped it. That recording could be the key to learning who was behind the attempts to kill them.

Of course, it could turn out to be nothing, too.

Lomax might have been lying when he gave them the info, but Lenora didn't think so. She figured the man wouldn't use his dying breath to lie, not when he could try to save his kid brother.

Clayton finished his latest call and sank down on the edge of the desk next to where she was sitting. "We got the search warrant, but it might be too late. Two FBI agents just showed up at the Abilene police department."

Lenora groaned and dropped the back of her head against the chair. "Dr. Landry must have told James about the recording."

He nodded. "Probably because he threatened or intimidated her."

Yes, but Lenora hadn't thought they could keep something like that a secret for long. Essentially it would be withholding evidence, maybe even obstruction of justice, and she couldn't imagine the doctor willingly becoming embroiled in something that could land her in jail. Still, Lenora wished that James hadn't managed to get agents over to Abilene P.D. so quickly.

"We do have something going for us," Clayton continued. "Several Abilene officers will accompany the FBI to conduct the search. So maybe James won't be able to have the recording hidden or destroyed, if that's what he was planning to do."

That was a big maybe. If James was the person on the recording, he would no doubt do whatever it took to make sure his guilt didn't come to light. If he was innocent, then they had nothing to worry about, because this could be a key piece of evidence that would blow the case wide-open.

Clayton turned the laptop in his direction and scanned through some emails. They'd been in the office for several hours now, and Lenora had noticed the email alerts popping onto the screen. Most were from Clayton's brothers, who were all working hard on the investigation. He clicked on the most recent email from Harlan, and she leaned in closer and read it along with him.

It wasn't good news.

Harlan still hadn't been able to get any info on the bank-account numbers that Quentin had given them.

"He hasn't been able to link the money to Melvin," Lenora mumbled. Yet another possible key piece of evidence that could still pan out.

"There might not be anything to link," Clayton reminded her. "The numbers could be bogus."

True, but if they did turn out to be real, that particular piece of evidence might confirm what was on the recording. And even if the account numbers didn't lead back to Melvin, that didn't mean the man was innocent.

Clayton looked at her and at the phone he'd just put back into his pocket. "Why don't you go ahead and get some rest?"

It wasn't that late, just past nine-thirty, but with the hellish events of the day, it felt a lot later. Of course, it'd been a while since she'd actually slept, and that was adding to the fatigue, too.

"The ranch is locked up tight," Clayton went on, "and the security system is set. The ranch hands are all armed and doing patrol. Around midnight I'll relieve Cutter so he can rest." Clearly, he was trying to convince her to go to bed.

Alone.

Lenora nearly stood and did as Clayton had said. But then she saw him glance at his phone again, and she frowned. "What are you planning to do?"

She saw the debate go through his eyes, and Lenora kept her stare firm. "I'm calling Melvin," he finally admitted.

Well, that certainly seemed safer than some of the other possibilities that had gone through her mind— like Clayton going to Abilene to keep an eye on the agents James had sent to retrieve the recording. She didn't want him anywhere near James, but more important, she didn't want him away from the ranch. Right now it seemed the safest place for both of them to be, especially since two of his brothers, Declan and Wyatt, were there, as well.

"You think Melvin might confess to receiving money for the hired guns?" she asked.

He lifted his shoulder and gave a weary huff. "No."

That's exactly what she figured. "Then don't put yourself through that. Just wait until some of the other evidence comes through for us, and maybe that evidence will be what you need to arrest Melvin." Lenora paused. "It will be so much easier if Melvin is guilty."

Clayton made a sound of agreement. "Arresting him would give me a certain satisfaction." But he shrugged. "It wouldn't change things, though."

"Would you want to change things?"

He blinked, maybe surprised that she'd want to launch into a discussion about their old baggage. She didn't. Not really. But old baggage had a way of making it into the present.

"Rocky Creek Children's Facility was a bad place," he said, obviously thinking about his answer. "But if I hadn't been there, I wouldn't have met my brothers. Or Kirby. I wouldn't be here at the ranch."

"Your home." Yes, it was stating the obvious, but she hated to see the past still able to hurt him this way.

"What about you?" he asked. "Would you go back and change things?"

"Absolutely." And she didn't even have to think about that. "I would have loved to have known my father. Even if he turned out to be, well, like yours. At least I'd know who he was."

Clayton stayed quiet a moment. "That's why you didn't keep the pregnancy a secret from me."

"That was a big part of it, yes," she admitted. And how could she say this without making it sound like an invitation for more? "But I also thought you'd be a good father."

"I will be," he promised her. But almost immediately he shook his head. "Better than I've been so far. I've done a lousy job of keeping you and the baby safe."

"Not so lousy. We're all alive." Sheesh. That sounded a little invitational, too. Best to move on to something not so personal.

Lenora stood. "How bad is your headache?"

He didn't get up from the desk, but that brought his gaze to hers. "Is it that obvious?"

Now it was her turn to shrug. "You haven't taken any meds in hours, so I figured there was pain."

"It's manageable," he said, and he caught her hand and eased her in front of him.

For a moment she thought Clayton might take her up on one of those *invitations* and pull her into his arms, but he didn't. He just stared at her. "You might find this hard to believe, since we had a one-night stand, but I'm pretty old-school when it comes to relationships and family."

Now she was the one who was surprised. She wasn't exactly sure where this conversation was going, but judging from the way Clayton was staring at her, it was going in a direction she might not like.

"You're not planning to challenge me for custody?" she asked.

"No." He repeated it, as if the idea hadn't even occurred to him.

While that was a relief, there was no relief in that it took him the longest moments in history to continue. "I've been giving this a lot of thought, and I feel the best thing is for us to get married and raise this baby together."

Lenora's mouth dropped open.

"Just hear me out," Clayton said before she could speak. Not that she would have known what to say, anyway. There were only a few times when she'd been rendered speechless, but this was one of those times.

"You and I both had some strikes against us right from the start," he explained. "Broken homes and bad breaks. Well, I don't want that for our baby. I want him or her to have chances we didn't get by being raised in a home with both parents."

She replayed every word in her head, but she still wasn't sure where to start. Obviously, Clayton expected her to give him a resounding yes.

Something she couldn't do.

"You want a marriage of convenience?" Lenora clarified.

He opened his mouth, closed it, then mumbled some profanity. "You make it sound like it's something bad. We're attracted to each other. If we hadn't been, we would have never landed in bed."

No way could she argue with the attraction part, and Clayton had enough proof of the attraction by the intensity and frequency of their kisses. When close to each other, they had zero resistance.

And that was why Lenora stepped back and put some space between them.

If she allowed him to pull her into his arms, her brain would turn to toast, and this was too important a decision to be thinking with parts of her body that shouldn't have a say in this.

But Clayton obviously had other ideas.

He slid his hand around her waist and kissed her. Really kissed her. So hard and so long that when he finally pulled back, Lenora was speechless for a different reason. She didn't have the breath to form the words. Good thing words weren't needed when he returned to her mouth for another kiss.

Oh, no.

This was exactly what she was trying to avoid. Her body just melted. So did any resolve she had to resist him, and Lenora felt herself leaning in closer. Closer. Until, yes, she was once again in his arms. And worse, she kissed him right back.

She let that dreamy feel of pleasure slide right into her. It excited her body and soothed it all at the same time. She had no idea how Clayton managed to accomplish that with just a kiss, but he did it.

And then pulled back.

Lenora was so wound up in his arms that she nearly staggered when he stepped away. That wasn't her only reaction, either. Every part of her began to protest that she was no longer body to body with the man who made her burn.

With that fire roaring through her, he didn't just head for the door. He opened it and said the rest of what he had to say from over his shoulder.

"Just think about the proposal," he mumbled. "And let me know your decision."

CLAYTON SANK DOWN onto the foot of his bed and cursed a blue streak. Well, his proposal certainly hadn't gone as planned. Not that he'd planned it very well, but he'd figured that Lenora would at least be more receptive to the idea of marriage so they could raise their child.

Apparently not, though.

Because only seconds after he'd suggested that she think about it, she had been the one to hurry past him and head to the guest room. And she'd shut the door, too. He knew that because it was directly across the hall from his; he'd also heard her lock it.

And turn off the lights.

He supposed it was a good sign that she was getting some much-needed rest. Something he wouldn't get much of tonight. But he had a sinking feeling that he'd insulted Lenora. Definitely not his intention. Yeah, they weren't in love, but he'd thought she would be able to see past that and do what was best for the baby.

Clayton mentally repeated that.

Groaned.

Yep, he'd blown it, all right. Lenora wasn't the sort of woman to lean on a man, any man, even if he happened to be the father of her child.

Cursing his suddenly sour mood, their situation and anything else he could think of to curse, Clayton waited a few seconds for his temper to die down, then called Cutter to make sure everything was still secure.

"Thought you'd be getting some rest," Cutter greeted him.

"I'm about to." Well, he was about to go to bed, anyway. Clayton doubted that rest would come, with so much on his mind. "I'll keep my phone right next to me. Call me if there's any trouble."

"Will do," Cutter assured him.

"I'll be out to relieve you at midnight," Clayton added, and he hung up.

He considered calling Harlan next, just in case there'd been some kind of breakthrough with the recording, but it would only interrupt whatever his brother was doing. Calling Declan was out, too, because hopefully both he and Wyatt were resting so they could also do relief duty at midnight.

It was going to be a long night.

Clayton cursed that as well, and he dropped back on the bed. His head had barely touched the mattress, however, when there was a sharp knock at the door. Just one rap, and it flew open. He automatically reached for his gun, but stopped when he saw it was Lenora.

"What's wrong?" he asked, getting up. He hurried to the door and looked out into the hall. Empty. "Did you hear something?"

She shook her head. "My answer is no."

It took him a moment to realize which question she was answering, and he was pretty sure it wasn't *did you hear something?*

Nope.

This was about the badly worded, ill-timed marriage proposal. Clayton took a deep breath, trying to figure out how to fix things, but he didn't get the chance. Lenora shut the door, and in the same motion she wound her arms around his neck and she kissed him.

Whoa.

He sure hadn't seen that coming, but Clayton went right along with it. He pulled her to him and he kissed her right back.

The taste of her roared through him. Instant heat. And it got significantly hotter when they tried to get closer to each other. Body to body. Every part of her touching every part of him. Well, the important parts, anyway.

"This doesn't feel like a no," he mumbled against her mouth.

"No to the marriage proposal," she clarified. "Yes to this." But then she stopped, pulled back and looked him directly in the eyes. "You do want this, right?"

"More than my next breath." And he snapped her back to him to continue, and deepen, the kiss.

He forced himself to remember to stay gentle. Not easy to do with the heat boiling into a fierce need that his body was already demanding he satisfy. It was that thought that had him pulling back and looking at her.

"Is this okay?" And he hoped he didn't have to explain that he was asking about sex during pregnancy.

She was breathing through her mouth now, her breath gusting, and her face was flushed with arousal. "More than okay," she assured him, and she pulled him back to her for round two.

It was hard to stay gentle when Lenora lowered her hand to his chest. She unbuttoned his shirt and her wandering fingers were headed even lower, to the zipper of his jeans, when Clayton decided he had to get control of this situation. He couldn't drag her to the floor and take her rough and hard. He had to put a leash on the fire, so he pinned her wrists to the back of the door.

She made a small sound of protest but continued the scalding-hot kiss. And even though she could no longer unzip him, she kept touching him. With her body. Specifically, her breasts on his chest. She didn't stop there, either. Lenora ground her sex against him and nearly made him forget his promise to keep this gentle.

When Clayton got his eyes uncrossed, he scooped her up and took her to the bed. He eased her onto the mattress and took off his boots and the ankle holster that contained a small Smith & Wesson.

But again Lenora sped things up. With her hands now free, she yanked off his holster and shirt. They landed somewhere on the floor, and her clever mouth landed on his chest.

Then his stomach.

Hell. He wasn't just losing this battle, he was on the verge of surrendering.

Since he obviously couldn't slow things down, he went after her clothes. First her top, and then he peeled off her jeans. He froze when he saw her stomach. Not because it cooled the heat. Nothing could do that, but it was a reminder that it was the first time he'd seen her this naked.

Or at least the first time he could remember.

"I know. My body's not very attractive," she said in a breathy whisper.

"You're wrong. You're incredibly attractive." And that was a massive understatement. Every part of her was beautiful.

He kissed the tops of her breasts and then opened the front-hook bra and rid her of that so he could kiss her breasts the way he wanted. She made a sound of pleasure, a low, sensual moan that vibrated through his body. She also lifted her hips.

But that wasn't all.

She hooked her fingers around the tops of her panties and shimmied them off.

Oh, man.

He'd been crazy before that, but now he got a lot crazier, and he took his mouth from her breast so he could work his way down her body. To her stomach.

To their child.

Her baby bump probably shouldn't have aroused him, but it did. Of course, at this point everything about her was arousing, and he wished the need wasn't a raging fire so he could savor every inch of her. Later, he'd have to do better. Would have to spend more time just sampling and savoring. And despite the fact that this probably shouldn't be happening, he was pretty sure he wouldn't regret this.

Just the opposite.

His body was already planning a second round.

While his mouth was occupied with kissing her stomach, she went after his zipper again, and this time she not only managed to get it down, she reached inside and touched him.

That crossed his eyes again.

And it upped the urgency.

Thankfully, Lenora was on the same page of urgency with him, and she helped him get out of the jeans and boxers. Naked, he landed against her, and she wrapped her legs around him. All thoughts of gentleness and baby bumps flew right out of his head when he eased inside the heat of her body.

A memory riffled through his head. Of another time, another bed.

But the same woman.

Yeah, he remembered that, and it only fired up his body even more—something he hadn't thought possible.

It was a first for him. He'd never had sex without a condom, and he probably should have asked Lenora if he needed to put one on. But then she moved again, and logical thoughts like that went straight out the window.

"Finish this," she muttered, pulling him even deeper inside her.

Clayton couldn't have said no even if he'd wanted. He moved inside her, falling into a frantic rhythm. The battle was there to keep things gentle, and he managed it. Somewhat. When he felt her close to the edge, he gathered her into his arms and gave her what she needed to finish.

She made that sensual sound again when the climax racked through her body. And she tightened her grip on him. He didn't need much to go over that edge with her, and that did it. Clayton pushed into her one last time and let himself fall right along with Lenora.

Chapter Fifteen

Lenora barely had time to catch her breath before Clayton moved off her. She immediately felt the loss of his body heat.

And his touch.

She nearly pulled him right back on her, but then realized he'd likely moved for her own comfort and for the sake of the baby. But it hadn't been uncomfortable. Just the opposite. Every part of her was still humming and slack from the pleasure of the climax.

Clayton turned onto his side, facing her, and eased toward her so that the top of her head was tucked under his chin. It was definitely intimate, since they were butt naked and recovering from the aftermath of incredible sex.

Well, it had been incredible for her, anyway.

She'd wanted Clayton since the first time she'd laid eyes on him, and their other time together had been clouded with grief. This time there were clouds, too, but she'd had a hard time remembering them when he was inside her.

But the clouds returned.

So did the mental list of what they were facing. And no, another round of sex wasn't on that list. Or at least it shouldn't have been. Too bad there wasn't a cure for

Clayton Caldwell so she could concentrate on what had to be done.

Yes, definitely clouds.

They had to continue the investigation and also had to work out something on a personal level that didn't involve a marriage of convenience. She wanted Clayton in their baby's life. She was certain now that he wanted it, too, but Lenora was also afraid that once he fully recovered from his injuries, he might feel differently, that he might even resent being tied to a woman he didn't love.

And there had been no talk of love.

Not even a hint, and despite the craziness going on, there had been a time or two when he could have said he was falling for her. Or maybe just that one day he might be able to fall for her.

But nothing, other than that milquetoast proposal.

"I remember," he said.

Even though he'd whispered it, his voice seemed to echo through the otherwise silent room. Lenora froze for a moment, processing that, and then she pulled back so she could meet his gaze.

"How much do you remember?" she asked.

Lenora didn't know why she was afraid of the answer, but she was. Maybe because Clayton had realized that it had been nothing more than a one-night stand between them.

And that's what it had been.

Two people in shock and filled with grief over a woman's murder. Except Lenora had the sinking feeling that it had been more than that for her.

A lot more.

Despite her not seeing Clayton for two months after that, she hadn't been able to forget him, and she was reasonably sure that the pregnancy was only a part of that. Even if she hadn't become pregnant, she doubted she would have just been able to walk away and forget him. Even if that's exactly what she should have done.

"I remember *you*," he said, as if choosing his words carefully. He slid his hand between them and over her stomach. "I remember that night."

She waited, but he didn't add more. Certainly nothing about what he'd been feeling when they'd dragged each other off to bed.

And nothing about what he was feeling now.

"You should get some rest," he said, kissing the top of her head. He would have gotten up from the bed if she hadn't caught him by the arm.

"Okay, what's wrong? What did you remember?" Lenora demanded.

He looked down at her, his gaze skirting over her naked body. "That you were anxious to get out of there afterward."

That was true. But it hadn't been because she wanted to leave Clayton, but rather because she hadn't wanted to fall apart in front of him. Hard to explain that to a man when they'd just had sex.

"Leaving wasn't about you," Lenora settled for saying.

He stared at her. Apparently it was her turn to add more, but she must have waited too long because Clayton made a slight sound of frustration, broke out of her grip and started getting dressed.

"I have to relieve Cutter soon," he said with his back to her. He pulled on his boxers and jeans.

Enough of this. It was nearly two hours until he had to pull relief duty, and she wasn't going to let him get away until she'd had a chance to explain.

Lenora got to her feet, too, and whirled him around

to face her. "I'm not used to relying on anyone, okay? And I left your bed that night because I was afraid of what I might say to you."

There. She'd bared her soul, but Lenora knew this wasn't finished. No. Clayton wanted her to say the words that she'd been afraid she might blurt out that night. However, he didn't have time to press her, because something else snagged his attention.

A shout.

It sent Clayton scrambling, first to turn off the lights, and then to the window. Since Lenora was still naked, she didn't immediately follow him, but she did gather up her clothes so she could dress.

"What's happening?" she asked.

"I'm not sure, but some of the horses are loose. I think it was Cutter who shouted something."

Relief washed over her body. After everything else they'd been through, loose horses didn't seem like much of an issue.

Unless...

"Do you see anyone out there?" Lenora quickly put on her clothes. "Someone who could have let them out?"

He shook his head just as his phone buzzed. With his attention still fastened outside the window, he pulled his cell from his pocket and answered it.

"Cutter," he said. "What's going on with the horses?"

Lenora couldn't hear what the ranch hand said, but she also didn't see anything too extreme in Clayton's reaction. Just the same concern that had been there since this entire ordeal started.

"I'll have a look," Clayton told Cutter, and he ended the call.

Now, that immediately upped Lenora's concern. "You're going out there?"

He nodded, finished dressing. "Cutter and the other ranch hands haven't seen anyone, but I need to find out why the horses have broken the fence. It might be nothing," he quickly added. Probably because he saw the fear in her eyes.

"It could be Johnny Lomax," she reminded him just as quickly. "He could have come here to try to kill us."

Clayton brushed a kiss on her cheek. "If it's Lomax, I need to find him."

He strapped on his holster and took another gun from the nightstand drawer. He handed it to her. "I want you to stay inside this room, away from the window. I'll lock the downstairs door behind me and have one of my brothers rearm the security system. It's not monitored by a company, but the alarm will alert us if anyone tries to break in."

Lenora was already shaking her head before he even finished. "You need to have one of your brothers go outside with you."

"I will," he mumbled.

But she wasn't sure he was telling the truth. Still, she couldn't stop him. Besides, if it was Lomax or some other hired gun, then he needed to be stopped before he could shoot into the house.

"If I need to talk to you, I'll call the landline." He tipped his head to the phone on the nightstand. "Remember, stay put."

And with that warning, he was gone.

Lenora shut the bedroom door and locked it, but pressed her ear against it, listening to the sound of Clayton's footsteps. When she could no longer hear him, she went back across the room. Not in front of the window just in case someone did fire a shot, but off to the side so she could look out.

There were at least a dozen horses on the driveway in front of the house and in the side yard. The animals weren't just milling around, either. They were moving as if they'd been spooked, not really going anywhere, just running. Still, she held out hope that this would all turn out to be nothing. After all, horses probably got out on occasion, and maybe this was one of those benign occasions.

She spotted Clayton in the backyard, and he wasn't alone, thank God. Declan was with him. That meant Wyatt was no doubt inside and had rearmed the security. She guessed that he would stay with Kirby, Stella and the nurse. The housekeeper had already gone home, so that was one fewer person to be concerned about, if this did turn out to be something.

Lenora had to remind herself to breathe when her lungs started to ache, and as if protesting at her suddenly tight muscles, the baby kicked hard. She slid her left hand over her stomach to try to soothe him or her, but she kept the gun ready in her right.

Thanks to the security lights, she watched as Clayton and Declan made their way across the backyard and toward the fence that stretched out behind the barn. She remembered seeing horses in that part of the pasture when she and Clayton talked to Quentin, but she couldn't see any back there now. Only the ones that were running free.

Her breath stalled again when she saw Clayton and Declan pivot toward the front of the house. Both took aim. But then just as quickly, they lowered their guns when Cutter came into view.

Good.

Not only wasn't it the threat that her body anticipated, but now Clayton had two people with him. She wished he had an entire army, because she had a very uneasy feeling about this.

Was Johnny Lomax out there?

The three men kept moving toward the back pasture. All stayed vigilant, with their gazes firing around them and their guns ready. It wasn't long, however, before they disappeared from view. What little peace of mind she had disappeared, as well. It sent her heart racing to know that Clayton could have to face down a killer out there in the darkness.

Lenora considered hurrying to another room with a rear-facing window so she could keep watch, but Clayton had told her to stay put, and that's what she would do. Besides, her movements might alarm Wyatt, and she didn't want to distract him, since he was likely keeping watch, too.

Since she couldn't see Clayton and the others, she tried to steady the heartbeat in her ears so she could hear what was going on. There were certainly no voices. No more shouts. Only the sound of the horses' hooves chopping into the ground below her. The quiet didn't lull her into a sense of safety, but she started to relax just a little.

When the sound pierced through the room.

But not just the room.

The shrill noise blasted through the entire house. And it was a sound she definitely hadn't wanted to hear. Not a shot. In some ways, this could be worse.

Because someone had set off the security alarm.

God, was the killer inside the house?

CLAYTON CURSED the moment he heard the alarm. The only way for it to be clanging like that was for someone to have opened a door or window. And since he'd

warned all of them—Lenora, Kirby, Stella and Wyatt—
not to leave, that meant one of them hadn't listened.

Or someone had broken in.

Hell, Lenora and the others could be in danger.

Clayton took out his cell and called the house phone,
as he'd promised Lenora he would do. She answered on
the first ring.

"What's going on?" Lenora immediately asked.

She was alive, thank God, and from the sound of it,
terrified. That wasn't good, but he'd take terrified over
wounded any day.

"I'm not sure what set off the alarm," Clayton answered. Or more like *who* set it off. "Are you okay?"

"Yes. Are you?"

"Fine." For now. He wasn't about to say that to her,
though. "Keep the bedroom door locked and stay away
from the window," he repeated. "I'll get there as fast
as I can."

He hung up, but not before he heard Lenora say, "Be
careful."

Clayton motioned for Declan and Cutter to follow
him when he started for the house. He ran, trying to
keep watch around him. After all, there was a possibility that the alarm had been tripped to draw them into an
ambush, but that was an outside chance. There'd been
opportunity for someone to shoot at them the minute
Declan and he had stepped outside.

But how had someone gotten past the ranch hands
and into the house?

With that question burning in his mind, Clayton ran
to the back porch. No one was in sight, and he couldn't
hear anything over the alarm. He tested the knob.

Locked.

Just as he'd left it.

He fished out his key from his pocket, opened the door and peered inside the kitchen. The room was practically pitch-black, also as he'd left it, and he couldn't see anyone lurking in the shadows. He reached inside and glanced at the security panel.

Clayton cursed again.

The tiny blinking red light stabbed through the darkness, an indication of which sensor had been tripped, and it was the sensor for a window in the den. The bottom floor of the house. He wasn't sure how an intruder had gotten past the ranch hands, but maybe the person had used the horses for a distraction. If so, it had worked.

"You think he's still outside the window?" Declan whispered, looking in at the light, as well.

Clayton shook his head. "He's inside." No way would a trained killer loiter around out there when the ranch hands were patrolling. He'd likely come with some kind of tool to break in and had gotten in fast.

Despite that horrible realization, Clayton didn't go barreling in. Too risky. He couldn't allow himself to be shot, because then he couldn't protect the others. But he didn't dawdle, either. It might have been a relief if someone had immediately shot at them. To have it over and done. And it would also mean the person wasn't anywhere near Lenora on the second floor. But that didn't happen, and it meant that someone was in another part of the house.

Maybe near Kirby, Stella and Wyatt.

Maybe headed upstairs.

Since it was on the way to the stairs, Clayton went to Kirby's room first and listened for any sounds to indicate where the intruder was. Nothing. In fact, no sounds at all. He tested the knob, which should have been locked.

It wasn't.

Hell, there was no way Wyatt would have unlocked the door unless there'd been some kind of emergency.

Even in the darkness, Clayton saw the alarm in Declan's eyes. "Keep watch," Clayton instructed Cutter, and he opened the door.

At first Clayton didn't see anything, until he looked at the floor. His heart went to his knees when he saw Wyatt, Stella and Kirby. Not moving. All in crumpled heaps.

Declan rushed in, and he immediately touched his fingers to Wyatt's neck. "He's alive. He's been stunned or something."

Definitely not good. It meant someone had gotten close enough to do that. But at least Wyatt was alive. Maybe Kirby and Stella, too.

While Clayton wanted to help Declan check the others, his first priority was Lenora and the baby. If the intruder had done this to Wyatt, Stella and Kirby, then he could have done it to Lenora.

Or worse.

He didn't let himself think of the *or worse,* but God knew what a stun gun would do to an unborn child. As a minimum, it could cause Lenora to miscarry.

Praying that he wasn't too late, Clayton hurried toward the stairs. He hadn't even made it to the first step when he saw something. A blur of motion. Someone dressed in dark clothes. He took aim but didn't fire, because he couldn't take the chance that it was Lenora trying to escape.

"Lenora?" he risked calling out to her.

"There's someone in the house," she shouted.

She was alive. He thanked God for that, too, but then he heard more movement. Not from the guest room where he'd left Lenora. No. This was much closer. Somewhere at the top of the stairs.

Clayton adjusted his aim and moved closer to the railing before he started up the steps. Shooting would be a huge risk, because bullets could go through the walls and hit Lenora.

That thought had no sooner crossed his mind when the shadowy figure darted out, and Clayton had only a split second to react. He dove to the side.

Just as the shot flew past him.

Chapter Sixteen

The shot was deafening. At first Lenora thought it'd been fired into her room. It took her a moment—one terrifying moment—to realize it'd been fired near the front of the house.

Where Clayton was now.

She opened her mouth to call out to him, to tell him to get down, but Lenora reminded herself that he was a lawman. Well trained in situations just like this. That didn't help. She could only think about him being hurt.

And that ripped her heart to shreds.

She couldn't lose him.

Still, if she called out to him, it might only make things worse. It could distract him at the worst possible time.

So far, all the attacks had been aimed at both her and Clayton, and Lenora didn't believe things would change now. Their attacker was no doubt trying to neutralize Clayton, and then he would come after her.

She had to fight every instinct in her body to save Clayton, but Lenora moved away from the door. Away from the window, too. And she got her gun ready in case she had to fire and defend herself.

Her hands were shaking. Not a little bit, either. She tried to get control of herself. It wouldn't do Clayton or her any good if she didn't think like an agent. Of course, the problem with that was she was a pregnant trained agent, and she couldn't get past the reminder that both her baby and her baby's father were in danger.

More shots.

They were all still centered near the front of the house. By the staircase, she guessed. Again, much too close to Clayton.

Judging from the rhythm of the shots, it wasn't just their attacker firing, but also Clayton returning fire. It sickened her to think of him being in the middle of a gunfight, and she prayed at least one of his brothers was there with him for backup.

Even with the deafening sound of the bullets, Lenora heard something else. Something she definitely didn't want to hear.

The doorknob rattled.

She hoped it was just a vibration from the shots, but then it jerked violently. No vibration. Someone was trying to get inside the bedroom.

"Clayton?" she risked asking. She scurried to the opposite side of the room, just in case the person on the other side was about to send a bullet in the direction of her voice.

"Stay down!" Clayton shouted to her.

It definitely wasn't him outside the door. Judging from the sound of his warning, he was still near the stairs. And unless the gunman was both shooting at Clayton and trying to get into the room with her, that meant there were two attackers.

At least.

God knew how many men had been sent after them to finish a job that'd been started months ago at the diner.

Another sound shot through the room. Not bullets.

But the ring of the house phone. She didn't dare risk answering it, because it could be a trick to pinpoint her location. After nearly a dozen rings, the phone finally went silent.

There were more gunshots, and someone shouted something that she couldn't make out. Not Clayton's voice, but not a stranger's, either. She thought it might have been Declan. Good. Maybe he was close enough to Clayton to help him put an end to this.

The doorknob rattled again, and Lenora moved to the far corner of the room, near the adjoining bath. There were no windows in there. No way to escape, either, once she was inside, but if the shooter made it through the door, she might be able to lock herself in so she could be in a better position to return fire.

Not that she wanted to do that.

But she wasn't just going to stand there and let someone gun her down, either.

Another rattle of the doorknob, and she heard the sharp sound of someone kicking at the wood. It took several hard kicks, and the hinges seemed to groan. When they gave way, the door flew against the wall.

The person came inside.

Lenora made a split-second assessment of the person who'd just knocked down the door. It wasn't Clayton or any of his family. It was someone dressed all in black, wearing a ski mask, and what the clothes and mask didn't conceal, the dark hallway did. She had no idea who this person was.

But she fired.

Not a kill shot, but she went for his shooting hand.

She missed.

The attacker was already moving to the side before she pulled the trigger, so her shot slammed into the jamb, right where he'd been just moments earlier. The person landed on the floor, out of her line of sight. Which meant she was out of his, too, but that wouldn't last for long.

"Lenora!" Clayton called out.

The hail of gunfire in the hall became even more fierce. Louder. Practically nonstop. Probably because Clayton was trying to fight his way to her. Lenora prayed he could do that, but she had to take measures of her own just in case one of their attackers managed to hold him at bay.

"I'm okay," she shouted back to Clayton, but before she even said the second word, Lenora was already on the move. From the corner and into the bath.

It wasn't a second too soon.

The shot came directly at her, and it put her heart right in her throat. She ducked deeper into the bathroom and tried to pick through the gunfire to try to hear her attacker approaching.

But that wasn't what she heard.

She heard Clayton cursing through the bursts of gunfire. There was also a lot of movement. Not just in the bedroom, where she figured her attacker was closing in on her. But this movement was coming from the hall. Frantic footsteps. Shouts and more bullets.

Lenora glanced out to see if she could figure out what was going on, but another bullet came right at her. She had no choice but to pull back. Thankfully, the lower half of the wall was covered with a combination of marble and slate, so she ducked down, using it as a bullet-resistant shield.

She didn't want to fire randomly to keep this guy from advancing. For one thing, the bullet might go through the wall and hit Clayton. And for another, she didn't want to waste ammo. The Glock that Clayton had given her held fourteen rounds, but she'd already fired once and didn't have extra bullets. There was no telling how much longer they'd be in a fight for their lives, and she might need those rounds to get them safely out.

"Stay down, Lenora!" Clayton shouted.

The gunman in the bedroom moved closer and fired into the bathroom. Not one shot but four, one right behind the other. They came at her so fast that the only thing Lenora could do was hover against the slate and pray that none of the bullets would slam into her.

But just like that, the shots stopped.

She saw the shooter dart to the other side of the room, deeper into the shadows, and Lenora couldn't figure out why he'd done that. She levered herself up a little so she'd have a better shot, but the sound of the footsteps had her holding her position.

A moment later, Clayton came bursting into the room.

"Get down!" she yelled when she saw the shooter take aim at him.

Lenora took aim, as well. At the man who was about to kill Clayton.

And she fired.

CLAYTON FIGURED that bursting into the bedroom would be a huge risk, that he might be shot before he could even try to save Lenora. But he had to try. He couldn't let whoever was in the room with Lenora hurt her and the baby.

The only part of Lenora that he could see was her hand as it snaked out, but he had no trouble hearing the shot she fired. It blasted through the room.

And it wasn't the only one.

Their attacker fired, too. The shot came right at Clayton and bashed into the wall just above his head.

Clayton dove to the floor, took aim and fired again. This time the bullet hit the man squarely in the chest, but he didn't go down. The man staggered back, and just when Clayton took aim to fire a second shot, blinding light stabbed through the room and right into his eyes. Not a normal light, but some kind of strobe light.

The pain was instant and so strong that if he hadn't already been on the floor, it would have sent him to his knees. He had no choice but to scramble to the side of the bed, away from the light and out of position to fire another shot at their attacker.

"Clayton!" Lenora called out, and he heard her moving around.

"Shoot at me again, Lynnie, and your lover is a dead man," the guy said.

Despite the searing pain, Clayton immediately recognized his voice.

Quentin.

Along with the pain, anger roared through Clayton. No way was he going to let Quentin get away with this. Of course, Clayton would have felt the same no matter who this man was.

So now they knew who wanted them dead, but knowing who was behind the attacks didn't help him now. Clayton tried to get control of the pain, but the light continued to come right at him.

"Stay back, Lenora," Clayton warned her.

He couldn't see her exact position, but she was somewhere in the bathroom. Clayton didn't want her to leave cover or try to save him, because Quentin would be able to shoot them both. The man was no doubt going to try to do that anyway, but Clayton didn't want to make it easier for him.

Clayton blew out several hard breaths, hoping to ease the torture in his head. "I shot you in the chest," he said to Quentin.

"Yeah, you did. Not too happy about that, because I'll have a hell of a bruise and it's burning like crazy."

Which meant Quentin was wearing Kevlar. Clayton wished he'd gone for a head shot, and if he got a second chance, that's exactly what he would do.

"I don't know what you're planning, but don't expect any help from your hired gun," Clayton managed to say. "I took out Johnny Lomax. He's dead at the top of the stairs."

"I figured as much, or you wouldn't have made it this far." If he was concerned about the loss of his hired gun, it didn't show in Quentin's voice.

"Lynnie," Quentin warned again, and this time there was emotion in his voice. Pure, raw anger.

"Please, don't," Clayton managed to say to her.

Clayton tried to get closer to her so he could shield her with his body, but Quentin just adjusted the strobe so that the jabs of light came right at Clayton. It was more effective than gunfire in neutralizing him. Worse, the pain was affecting his vision. Everything was a blur. He had to be able to see Quentin so he could take him out.

"Clayton, we got a problem," he heard Declan shout out. "A big one."

That was *not* what Clayton wanted to hear. Before he'd barreled into the guest room to try to save Lenora, he had left Declan standing guard in the entry at the bottom of the stairs. With the security system off, Clayton hadn't wanted anyone else to sneak in. Cutter was with Stella, Kirby and Wyatt while they regained consciousness from what was probably a stun gun attack. Clayton prayed that Quentin hadn't sent a henchman to hurt any of them, but obviously something had gone wrong.

"Go ahead, Marshal. Tell Clayton what the problem is," Quentin called out to Declan, and he sounded very pleased with himself. "I think your brother will want to hear just what kind of *help* I brought with me."

Quentin was actually enjoying this, and Clayton wished he could beat the man to a pulp for being so cavalier about putting so many lives in danger.

"With all the gunfire, I didn't hear them come in until it was too late," Declan said. Unlike Quentin, there was nothing but concern in his brother's voice. "Three men. One is holding a gun on me, and the other has a gun aimed at the ceiling."

"Not just any ordinary gun, either," Quentin volunteered. "It's a high-powered automatic loaded with armor-piercing bullets."

From the sound of it, Clayton figured it was a machine gun. Definitely not something he wanted in the mix of this battle with Quentin.

"Oh, and the triggerman doesn't have it aimed at just any ceiling," Quentin added. "He has it pointed right at the bathroom floor where Lenora is standing."

Hell. And with armor-piercing bullets, the shots would tear through the floor and hit her.

Lenora shifted her position, obviously getting ready to move.

"I wouldn't advise that, Lynnie," Quentin told her. "My triggerman and I are wearing communicators, so he can hear every word I say. And here's what I'm telling him. If he hears another shot or any kind of movement, he's to start firing. You'd be dead before you could draw your next breath."

Chapter Seventeen

Lenora froze. She glanced down at the floor where she was standing. It wasn't hard for her to picture Quentin's lackey beneath her, his gun ready to blow her to bits.

She wanted to curse Quentin and put an end to this, but she couldn't risk firing a shot, because it could get both Clayton and her killed. Especially since that blasted light had essentially disarmed Clayton. God knew how much pain he was in, and all because of Quentin.

"Why are you doing this?" she asked Quentin. But she didn't really care why. She just wanted to figure out a way to get Clayton and his family out of this.

"I thought that was obvious. Revenge. No way could I let you get away with what you did to me. Spying on me. Giving that SOB Agent Britt all the dirty little details of my life."

Quentin adjusted the light, and even though she couldn't see Clayton, she supposed Quentin was doing that to torment him. Without the gunfire, Lenora could hear Clayton's muffled sounds of pain.

"What I did to you?" she repeated. "You were breaking the law, and you were using me to do it."

"You knew exactly what you were doing," Quentin fired back.

But she hadn't known about the criminal activity

until James had shown up at her home and told her. Of course, in Quentin's crazed mind, maybe blaming her was what he needed to do to justify his own guilt.

"Okay, here's how this is going to work," Quentin continued. He also continued slashing that light at Clayton. "You're both going to put down your weapons. Carefully, and keeping your hands where I can see them. And then Lynnie's going to step out and come with me."

Oh, God. He was planning to kidnap her. Or maybe that was just a ruse to get her to leave cover. Quentin could just shoot and kill her first chance he got.

"Oh, and if you don't drop your guns," he went on, "then my second and third triggermen have orders to shoot. He'll start with your brother by the stairs and then move on to the others in the back bedroom."

Clayton didn't respond to that right away, but she heard him take several more of those forced breaths. "Declan, where's Wyatt, Cutter and the others?"

"Can't tell, but I'm guessing they're being held at gunpoint." Declan paused. "But Harlan, Dallas and Slade are on the way."

Lenora had no idea if that last part was true. She prayed it was. They could definitely use the backup from three marshals, but the question was—if Declan had managed to contact his brothers and inform them of the attack, would they arrive in time?

"Put your guns on the floor," Quentin ordered again. "You first, Lynnie."

She didn't rush to do that. Instead, she leaned out just a little so she could take in the entire room. Well, what she could see of it, anyway. The strobe light was blaring on Clayton, who was trying to shield his eyes from it, but it also made the rest of the room—including where Quentin was standing—hard to decipher.

"How did you get inside the house?" Lenora asked Quentin. She wanted him talking so she could try to figure out what to do.

He made a sound to indicate that was obvious. "It's easier to keep track of everyone when one of my men has infrared. We knew when to sneak into the pasture and let out the horses. To create a distraction. Like what you're trying to do to me now. Put your gun on the floor."

The anger in Quentin's voice went up a significant notch. He obviously wasn't going to fall for her tricks. Still, surrendering her weapon was a huge risk. No way for her to return fire if she did that.

"Do as he says," Clayton told her.

Even though she couldn't see Clayton's face, she knew he wouldn't want her to give Quentin's trigger-man a reason to start firing. So Lenora stepped in the doorway of the bathroom and stooped so she could put the gun on the floor.

"Kick it across the floor, away from your lover," Quentin instructed.

It was the second time Quentin had referred to Clayton as her lover. Maybe because he knew that Clayton was her baby's father. Or maybe there was another reason.

A sickening one.

It was possible that Quentin had used the infrared he mentioned to watch them have sex. Of course, he wouldn't have been able to actually see them with the infrared, but Quentin could have figured it out. She hated that he had violated her in so many ways.

Lenora pinned her attention to Quentin and gave her gun a kick. It landed by the edge of the bed. Out of her reach, but Clayton might still be able to dive for it.

"Good girl," Quentin said in that mocking tone. "Now, Clayton, it's your turn. Put your gun on the floor and shove it toward me."

Clayton leaned forward, but he didn't let go of his gun. "What are you going to do with Lenora?"

"I'm surprised you'd want to hear all the dirty little details." Quentin didn't wait for Clayton to respond. "In a nutshell, I'm going to make her pay for what she did. And I need time and privacy for that."

It turned her stomach to think of what Quentin wanted to do to her. She wanted to fight back now, but it was too big a risk to take with the gunman below her. Maybe once they were out of the room she'd have a better chance of escaping, because there was no way she could leave the ranch with this man who wanted to torture her.

Quentin cursed. "Must I keep repeating myself? Put your gun on the floor."

Clayton moved again. Just a little. Clearly, he was trying to stall, so Lenora helped him out by asking Quentin another question. She didn't care what the answer was, but she wanted to buy Clayton some time.

"Why would you possibly work for a man like Riggs?"

"I'm not," Quentin quickly denied. "In fact, Riggs refused to fund this little adventure. Thought it was a setup of some kind."

If their lives weren't on the line, it would have been a relief to hear that, but it didn't lessen the danger to know that Jill's killer wasn't involved.

"All that bank account info I gave you was just to muddy the waters," Quentin continued. "The gun, Clayton."

Clayton moved again and put his gun on the floor, but he didn't pull back his hand.

"So if it's me you want," Lenora said in a voice loud enough that hopefully Quentin would look at her, "then let Clayton and his family go."

"Impossible. You're carrying his family. No way can I leave Clayton alive."

"He's right," Clayton confirmed. "I'd come after him, and I'd find him. And kill him."

Lenora cringed. Clayton was throwing down a gauntlet, and she didn't miss the sound of outrage that Quentin made.

"Get your hand off that gun," he told Clayton, "or Lenora dies right now."

Clayton cursed. But he drew back his hand, and in the same motion he kicked the gun toward the foot of the bed. She prayed he had a backup weapon and that he'd be able to get to it if it came down to it.

"Good," Quentin said, but there was no real praise in his voice.

Quentin turned toward Lenora. "Come here, Lynnie." Because of the light, she still couldn't see his face, but she had no doubt that his attention held firmly on her.

"Do as he says," Clayton instructed.

When Lenora stepped out, she saw Clayton's hand move toward his boots, where he hopefully had some kind of backup weapon.

"Come closer," Quentin ordered.

Lenora did, and she tried to position her body in between the two men so that Quentin wouldn't be able to see what Clayton was doing. But that didn't last long, because the moment she was within Quentin's reach, he tossed the strobe light aside and grabbed her, slinging her in front of him.

Just the touch of his hand on her had her skin crawling, but at least the light was no longer stabbing into Clayton's eyes. Now that she could see Clayton's face, she could see the agony. He was in horrible pain, maybe too much to stop Quentin. And there was something else very bad about the new position. She was literally shielding Quentin, so that even if Clayton could return fire, he wouldn't have a clean shot.

Well, not until they moved.

And according to Quentin, he intended to move her, to take her elsewhere so he could punish her. For that to happen, they would have to walk out of the room, and maybe that's when Clayton could help her stop this.

"Here's how this is going to work." Quentin put his mouth right against her ear when he spoke, but he didn't whisper. He kept his voice loud enough for Clayton to hear. "I'm giving you a huge gift. An opportunity to keep your baby alive."

Lenora hated to latch on to the hope that Quentin was telling the truth, but she desperately wanted it to be true. "How?" she asked. And despite the pain, Clayton looked as skeptical as she felt.

"Easy," Quentin answered. "If you do just one little thing, I'll take you someplace safe, where you can finish your pregnancy and deliver the baby. I'll even have the kid sent back to Blue Creek Ranch, so he can grow up to be a cowboy like his daddy."

Quentin hadn't said a word about keeping her alive, but at the moment she was willing to do whatever it took for her baby's safety.

"What's the one little thing?" And she held her breath, waiting for an answer that she was certain she didn't want to hear.

Quentin took her hand and wrapped her fingers around his gun. "Easy. Kill Clayton and your baby lives."

HELL. WHAT KIND of sick game was Quentin playing now?

He was putting Lenora in an impossible situation. One no doubt meant to punish her. If Clayton had thought for one second that his death would allow Lenora and the baby to live, he would trade his life for theirs.

But he didn't trust Quentin.

No.

If Lenora went through with the shooting, then Quentin would only turn that gun on her or else kill her after he'd tortured her. To stop that from happening, Clayton needed a plan.

But what?

If the pain would stop roaring in his head, he might be able to come up with one. Unfortunately, that strobe light had done a real number on him, but he tried to force himself to think through the pain.

He was sure his other brothers were on the way from Maverick Springs. His cell phone had buzzed several times in the past fifteen minutes, and even though he hadn't risked looking at the screen, Clayton figured it was either Harlan, Dallas or Slade. One of them had probably tried to call the house phone, too, and when they hadn't gotten an answer, they would have driven out.

Hopefully Quentin didn't have other gunmen stashed outside to ambush them.

"Shoot him, Lynnie," Quentin demanded. He forced

her to move forward, toward the door and the hall. No doubt where he was planning to escape.

Lenora shook her head, and even through the pain, he could see the tears shimmering in her eyes. "Give me another option," she demanded right back.

Quentin laughed, but there was no humor in his tone. "You always were difficult. I would have killed you sooner, you know, but I couldn't find you when you went into hiding after Jill's murder."

That put a new height on the hatred Clayton felt for this piece of slime.

"If you'd wanted me dead, you could have just waited at my house, the one you vandalized," Lenora reminded him. "But I don't think you wanted to kill me. I think you wanted to torment me." Despite the tears, her voice was surprisingly strong.

Clayton wasn't sure that was a good idea.

He didn't want Lenora to do anything to provoke Quentin more. The man was obviously operating on a short fuse. So all Clayton needed was some kind of distraction. Just a few seconds, so he could draw the Smith & Wesson from his boot holster and blast Quentin to smithereens. Of course, for that to happen, he'd first have to get Lenora out of the way.

"Guilty," Quentin agreed. "I do love tormenting you." And with his gaze now fixed on Clayton, Quentin kissed Lenora on the cheek. "Wish I could drag this out a little bit longer, but I figure Clayton has reinforcements on the way, and you and I need to leave before they get to the house."

Quentin shoved her forward again. Closer to the door. And he lifted Lenora's hand, pointing the gun right at Clayton. "Put your finger on the trigger."

"No." And she tried to shove the gun away.

"Either put your finger on the trigger," Quentin warned, "or Clayton will get the pleasure of seeing me kill you where you stand."

It was the first thing Quentin had said tonight that Clayton believed. He would kill Lenora, and with the way their bodies were positioned, Clayton wouldn't have the shot to stop the man.

"Lenora?" Clayton called out. Just as he'd hoped, she quit struggling. He didn't want the gun to go off accidentally, because it could still kill her.

Her gaze came to his again, and she seemed to be waiting for him to give her some kind of signal. He wanted her to move out of the way, but he didn't see how she could safely do that. After all, Quentin had her hand clamped around the gun.

"Do you still want to marry me?" she asked. "If so, my answer is yes."

Clayton didn't know who was more stunned—Quentin or him. The timing certainly sucked, but Clayton thought the sucky timing was exactly what Lenora wanted. It was such a simple thing. Just a couple of sentences, but she must have known it would send Quentin into a jealous rage.

And it did, all right.

Quentin made a feral sound, and he latched on to Lenora's arm so hard that Clayton was sure that he was about to kill her on the spot.

But Lenora made her own sound—a loud screech, and she tore herself from Quentin's grip and dove toward the bed.

Just as the blast echoed through the room.

LENORA INSTINCTIVELY PUT her hands over her stomach to try to protect the baby, and she tried to scramble across the bed and to the floor.

She failed.

The shot came anyway, before she could protect herself. And she braced herself for the feel of the bullet slamming into her body.

That didn't happen, either.

Instead, the bullet went in Clayton's direction. Into the floor where he'd been only seconds before she'd started this whole distraction thing to get her away from Quentin. It'd been a gamble. A huge one. And she was counting heavily on Clayton having some other weapon. If not, well, they were both about to die.

From the corner of her eye, she saw Clayton roll to the side, and when he came up, he had a gun in his hand.

Thank God.

He fired at Quentin, but just as Clayton had done, he got out of the path of the oncoming bullet. Quentin landed in the doorway, part of him in the bedroom and the other part in the hall.

The shots came instantly. A battering of bullets that nearly felt like an earthquake. It took her a moment to realize that neither Quentin nor Clayton had fired the shots, but instead they'd come from below.

Her stomach twisted into a knot.

Quentin had warned them if shots were fired, then his goon downstairs would try to kill them. And that's exactly what he was trying to do. The bullets began to blast their way through the bathroom floor.

However, those weren't the only shots she heard. There were others downstairs. Maybe from Declan or maybe from Clayton's other brothers. She hadn't heard a vehicle approaching the ranch house, but with everything going on, she could have easily missed it. If so, there could be a life-and-death fight going on one floor beneath them.

She thought of Kirby, of how sick he was. Too sick to fight back. And maybe he wasn't even conscious yet. He, Stella and Wyatt could be sitting ducks right now, and she doubted the gunmen would show any mercy and keep any of them alive.

"Stay on the bed," Clayton yelled to her. And he came off the floor and took aim at Quentin.

The man skittered out of sight. Somewhere in the dark hall. But Lenora was betting he wouldn't go far. No. He wouldn't give up yet, because it would mean his arrest for attempted murder and God knew how many other charges. That made him beyond desperate and very dangerous.

The bullets from below ate their way through the bathroom floor and into the ceiling. And then the angle changed. God, no. The shooter had moved, maybe because Quentin had told him through the communicator, but now the floor shots were going in Clayton's direction.

Lenora reached down to pull him onto the bed with her. Not that the mattress and frame would give them much protection, but it was better than nothing. And besides, the bed was aligned with the door, so that they might be able to spot Quentin.

A bullet rammed into the metal bed frame. She heard the plinging sound. Felt it, too. The jolt. But she didn't have time to dwell on it.

She had to try to save Clayton.

Clayton scrambled onto the end of the mattress, and he positioned himself in front of her. Shielding her in case Quentin came through the door again. But as frightening as that prospect was, Lenora was terrified that the gunman below would get lucky with those blind shots. Heck, it wouldn't even take much luck because of the sheer volume of bullets that were coming their way.

"He's behind you!" she heard Declan yell.

And she held her breath, praying that none of Clayton's family had been hurt.

There was another blast, different from the shots going into the floor. And just like that, that battery of bullets stopped. The room suddenly became so quiet that the only sound she could hear was her own heartbeat crashing in her ears.

"All clear down here," Declan shouted.

Lenora released the breath she'd been holding and was beyond thankful that the floor shooter was out of commission. But Quentin was no doubt alive and ready to launch round two.

"Clayton, are you okay?" It was Declan again. From the sound of his voice, he was making his way up the stairs.

Clayton didn't answer Declan, though. He took aim at the door. Waiting.

"Get in the closet," Clayton whispered to her.

Lenora hated to leave him to fight this battle alone, but she had to think of the baby. She couldn't risk it, so she scrambled off the bed and reached down to scoop up her gun. However, she didn't even make it a step toward the closet when she saw the blur of motion from the corner of her eye.

The sound came with it.

Yelling at the top of his lungs, Quentin ran into the room, his gun already aimed not at her but at Clayton. Clayton ducked to the side and they both fired at the same time. Even though she couldn't see if Clayton had been hit, Lenora saw the bullet tear through Quentin's arm.

It didn't stop him.

He squeezed the trigger, his shots blistering through the air, and Lenora dropped to the floor when one of them bashed into the headboard.

She pivoted and took aim at Quentin. But it was already too late. Lenora shouted for Clayton to get down, but it was too late for that, as well.

Quentin fired.

So did Clayton.

And this time he didn't hit Quentin in the chest or shoulder. The shot went into his head. Quentin seemed to freeze. For a split second his gaze met hers, and then he crumpled to the floor.

The shock paralyzed her for several moments, but then she hurried to Clayton to make sure he was okay. But the look on his face let her know that he wasn't.

"You're hurt," Lenora said.

Clayton frantically shook his head. "No. But you are."

Lenora had no idea what he meant, but then she looked down and saw the blood on the front of her shirt.

Oh, God.

Maybe it was the blood or something else, but Lenora suddenly felt woozy. The room started to spin, and she could barely make out Clayton's face.

However, she heard his voice.

"I'm getting you to the hospital now." He scooped her up in his arms and started running.

Chapter Eighteen

"She'll be okay," Clayton heard his brother Wyatt say to him.

Wyatt wasn't the first family member to try to reassure him that Lenora would get through this. So had Harlan and Declan, who were now on the phone trying to get an update on the investigation wrap-up. Kirby, too, had tried to give Clayton some reassurance before the medics had taken him up the hall of the Maverick Springs Hospital to be checked out.

Even though Kirby had arrived in an ambulance, he thankfully didn't appear to have any serious injuries. Ditto for Clayton's brothers and Stella. No injuries.

But Lenora was a different matter.

She'd been in the examination room with Dr. Landry for what seemed an eternity now, but after checking the time, Clayton realized it had been less than a half hour.

Clayton would have gone in with them, but the doctor had said she needed to give Lenora a thorough exam. Yeah, Lenora and he had been intimate, twice, but he doubted Lenora would want him in there for that. And that meant he had to wait while everything inside was yelling for him to make sure she was all right.

He didn't know how bad her injuries were, but there'd

been blood, so Lenora had likely been shot. That meant both the baby and she could still be in danger.

How the hell could he have let this happen to her?

She'd put her safety in his hands, and he'd failed her in the worst kind of way.

Clayton cursed Quentin, and even though the man was dead, it didn't lessen his anger. Quentin's jealousy and need for revenge had caused four of his hired guns to be killed, it'd put Clayton's entire family at risk and it would give him enough nightmares to last a lifetime. He'd never forget seeing that blood on Lenora's shirt and the terrified look in her eyes when they'd come under attack.

Declan finished the phone call he was making, and all of them turned toward him to hear what, if anything, he'd learned.

"That was Agent James Britt." Declan kept his attention nailed to Clayton. "They found the recording at Lomax's sister's house. Just where Lomax said it would be. It confirms that Quentin did indeed hire the gunmen to come after you and Lenora."

Well, that tied up everything in a neat little package. *Maybe.* "Any signs that James had anything to do with this?"

Declan shook his head. "But he just rattled on about how sorry he was that Lenora nearly got killed. I don't think he's dirty, but I think he knows he did a lousy job with the way he handled things, including the time when she worked for him as a CI."

A lousy job was right, but Clayton would take that over a dirty agent, and it was looking as if James was no longer a suspect in any of this. Later, when he saw the agent, he would apologize for suspecting him. And that brought him to the next question.

"Any chance that Melvin had a part in Quentin's plan?" he asked Declan.

"Sorry, but no. I was looking forward to arresting him for something, but looks like we'll have to wait. There's no proof whatsoever that Quentin or Riggs hired Melvin to do anything wrong."

Yeah. But Clayton didn't know how hard he'd be looking into Melvin's dirty dealings. If Lenora made it through this and both she and the baby were okay, then Clayton wanted to focus on them and not the man who'd been part of his past. Strange that it had taken something like nearly losing Lenora to put things in perspective.

Clayton again looked at the door to the room where she was being examined, and again he considered going in there. He wasn't sure how much longer he could wait to learn how she was doing. And even though this conversation about the wrap-up of the investigation was important, nothing was more important than Lenora.

"That brings us to Riggs," Harlan added. He, too, had finished a phone call just shortly before Declan's. "The FBI and the sheriff aren't finding anything to link Riggs to this, but the justice department used this latest incident to prove to a federal judge just how dangerous Riggs could be, even behind bars. So they finally got approval to freeze all of Riggs's assets. That should stop him if he decides to hire someone to deter Lenora and you from testifying."

Yet more good news. They wouldn't have to spend the next few months looking over their shoulders. But it wasn't the good news that Clayton needed to hear.

He whirled around when he heard the footsteps headed toward the waiting room, but it wasn't Dr. Landry. It was another doctor, Tony Reardon, who was new to Maverick Springs.

"You're Kirby's son?" he asked, pinning his gaze to Clayton.

"We all are." Clayton motioned to Dallas, Wyatt, Slade, Declan and Harlan. "How is he? And Stella?"

"They're both fine," the doctor answered. "Stella got a bump on her head when she fell after being hit with the stun gun."

Clayton looked back at Wyatt, who confirmed that with a nod. "Kirby was in bed, so he didn't hit the floor."

The doctor frowned and looked up at the bruises on Wyatt's cheek and forehead. "Is that what happened to you?"

"I'm okay," Wyatt insisted, not answering the question, but he'd already told Clayton that the two gunmen had bashed their way through Kirby's bedroom window and first grabbed Stella to use her as a human shield. They'd hit Wyatt with a projectile stun gun, then they'd hit Kirby and Stella. They hadn't even had a chance to fight back.

The doctor made a sound to indicate he didn't agree with Wyatt's *I'm okay* remark, and he looked at the chart that he was holding. "Stella can go home, but I want to keep Kirby for the night."

That didn't help steady Clayton's nerves.

"I thought you said he was all right," Harlan immediately protested.

"He is, but because of his existing condition, I want to keep an eye on him. He's hooked up to an IV right now, and I'd like to get more fluids in him."

Kirby wasn't going to like that, but in this case, Clayton was on the doctor's side. Better safe than sorry, and heaven only knew what the stress had done to Kirby's already-weak body.

"What about Lenora?" Clayton asked. He knew Dr.

Reardon hadn't examined her, but he was desperate for news.

"She has the gunshot wound, right?" the doctor said looking at the chart again.

That did it. Clayton was already operating on a short fuse, and just hearing *gunshot wound* was the last straw. He went to the door where Dr. Landry had taken Lenora and he knocked once. But he didn't even wait for a response. He threw it open.

And his heart went to his knees.

Clayton had hoped to see Lenora sitting up, but the room was dusky dark, and she was lying down on the examining table. Her top was off, discarded onto the back of a chair, and Dr. Landry had a needle jammed into the top of Lenora's shoulder.

"I couldn't wait," he said, shutting the door behind him. "I had to know."

Lenora managed a smile and reached out her hand to him. It took him a moment to get his feet moving, because just looking at her pale face brought back all the memories of the attack.

Of just how close he'd come to losing her.

Clayton went to the examining bed and brushed a kiss on her mouth. It didn't help soothe him, but Lenora made a soft sound of, well, something. Probably not pleasure. Relief maybe. And she tightened the grip she had on his hand.

"I'm fine, really," she tried to assure him, but words weren't going to give him much reassurance. He had to see for himself that she was okay, and so far what he was seeing only confirmed that she had indeed been shot.

"The bullet sliced through the top of her shoulder," Dr. Landry explained. "Not much damage, just a flesh wound. She's already stitched up, but I was just giving her a little extra local anesthesia for the pain."

"You're in pain?" Another stupid thing to say. Of course she was. She'd been shot.

Lenora shook her head. "I didn't want to take any pain pills, so this will help when the numbness wears off. How are Kirby, Stella and Wyatt?"

"Fine." And he didn't want to discuss them. Clayton wanted to talk about how she was doing. He watched the doctor put aside the needle and pick up another piece of equipment.

"Is it okay if he stays for this?" the doctor asked Lenora.

Lenora looked up at him, and for a moment he thought she was going to ask him to leave, but she just nodded. "Dr. Landry's about to do an ultrasound."

He'd heard of them. Some kind of sonar imaging to see the baby. That didn't help the nerves, either. God, was something wrong with the baby?

"It's just a precaution," Lenora said, her voice a gentle whisper. "The baby's moving just fine, and Dr. Landry says my injury wouldn't have any impact on the pregnancy."

He wanted to believe that. Desperately wanted to. But with all the bad things that had happened in the past couple of months, he was having a hard time hanging on to hope.

Dr. Landry helped Lenora put a scrub top on rather than her bloody shirt. Clayton didn't ever want to see that shirt again.

"Okay, let's get a look at this kid," Dr. Landry said. She pushed up the gray-green sheet that was covering Lenora. She was still wearing her jeans, but they'd been shoved down to her hips so that her belly was exposed.

The doctor used a squeeze bottle to smear some goopy-looking stuff over Lenora's stomach.

Clayton figured in just a few seconds, they'd all be caught up in seeing the baby. And that was critical. He had to know that his child was okay. But there was something else critical, too, and while he would have preferred this conversation to be private, he didn't want to delay it or the ultrasound.

He leaned in closer to Lenora. "You said yes, that you'd marry me."

She blinked, no doubt surprised that he'd bring it up now. "I did."

Instant relief. Well, sort of. She remembered saying it, but Clayton wanted more. Much more. "Did you mean it?"

She stared at him a moment while the doctor continued to get the machine ready for the ultrasound. "I meant it," Lenora verified. "But not for the reasons you think."

Okay, there went any sense of relief. "You said it to distract Quentin."

Another blink, and Lenora frowned. "No. I said it because I'm in love with you, and that's the reason I want to marry you."

Dr. Landry cleared her throat. "Uh, should I step out for a minute or two?"

"No," Lenora and Clayton said in unison. "Clayton and I can talk afterward. Go ahead and do the ultrasound."

But Clayton didn't want to wait until *afterward.* Partly because Lenora had knocked the breath out of him with what she'd said. "You're in love with me?"

Lenora smiled and pulled him down for a kiss. "Don't look so shocked. You're a very lovable guy."

Clayton hoped like hell that she wasn't toying with him, but he knew Lenora wasn't the toying type. In fact, he knew a lot about her.

"Good." He returned the kiss. "Because I'm in love with you, too."

Now it was Lenora's turn to look shocked. She made another sound, too—a breathy, happy sound that rushed right out of her mouth and against his when he kissed her again.

"You love me?" she asked.

"Hey, you're a very lovable woman." And because he couldn't help himself, he continued the kiss.

Until the doctor cleared her throat again. "I don't mind doing stitches or ultrasounds, but I'd rather not witness celebratory foreplay. Besides, those kisses are making Lenora squirm, and I need her to stay still for this."

Clayton smiled at the thought of making Lenora squirm, but he did as the doctor asked. However, it was darn hard not to kiss Lenora with her nuzzling her face against his. The nuzzling continued until the images popped up on the screen.

His breath stalled in his lungs.

It didn't look like a baby. More like some alien creature. He hadn't expected seeing those fuzzy images would pack such a wallop.

"Oh, man," Clayton mumbled, and he had no choice but to lean against the bed. He thought his legs might buckle at any second.

"Yes," Lenora whispered and clutched his hand again.

He had no doubt that she knew exactly what he was feeling. The love. The joy. The terror. Yeah, that, too. It suddenly seemed like such a huge weight to be responsible for that little life, but then Clayton felt no weight at all. Just the miracle of seeing his baby.

"Lots of movement," the doctor said, her attention on the screen.

"That's good?" Clayton asked once he could get his mouth to form words.

"Very good. Everything looks great. Fingers, toes, heartbeat…" But Dr. Landry's explanation ground to a halt, and she glanced back at them. "You want to know the sex of the baby?"

Clayton looked at Lenora to see how she felt about that, but she only shrugged. He was still debating it when he looked at the screen again and saw what had caught the doctor's eye. Even though the image was alien-like, Clayton had no trouble seeing *that*.

"Sorry, sometimes it's hard to conceal the sex," the doctor explained.

Apparently, Lenora saw it, too. "It's a boy," she mumbled. Her breath caught in her throat.

Clayton's breath caught, as well.

A son.

He would have been happy with either, but now that he knew they were having a boy, it was easier to see him. Not just as a baby, but growing up, too. He could be the father to this child that Kirby had been to him.

And better.

Because his son would have a better start to life than either of them had had.

"You'll change diapers?" Lenora asked, her joke cutting through the silence.

"Definitely." He'd walk through fire for both of them, and he let her know that with another kiss. And Clayton didn't care if this one was too hot and too long for the doctor to witness. Everything around him disappeared except for Lenora and their son.

"Good thing Lenora's already pregnant," the doctor mumbled, "or else she'd soon be that way."

That caused Lenora and Clayton to laugh. They had to break the kiss, temporarily, but they stayed wound around each other.

"I'm very happy," Lenora whispered against his mouth. "And in love with you."

"I'm very happy," Clayton repeated. "And in love with you, too."

"All right," the doctor said, putting aside the ultrasound device. She wiped the goop off Lenora's stomach and helped her pull her jeans back up. "This is getting a little too private for my ears. You can go ahead and take Lenora home—and to bed. But congrats. Sounds as if you two will be married before this little fella makes his way into the world."

Oh, yeah.

If Clayton had anything to say about it, they'd be married tomorrow. He didn't want to wait another minute to start his life with Lenora. Clayton scooped her up in his arms and started for home.

* * * * *

The Marshals of Maverick County continues next month! Look for OUTLAW LAWMAN by USA Today *bestselling author Delores Fossen wherever Harlequin Intrigue books are sold!*

COMING NEXT MONTH from Harlequin® Intrigue®
AVAILABLE JUNE 18, 2013

#1431 OUTLAW LAWMAN
The Marshals of Maverick County
Delores Fossen
A search for a killer brings Marshal Harlan McKinney and investigative journalist Caitlyn Barnes face-to-face not only with their painful pasts but with a steamy attraction that just won't die. Only together can they defeat the murderer who lures them back to a Texas ranch for a midnight showdown.

#1432 THE SMOKY MOUNTAIN MIST
Bitterwood P.D.
Paula Graves
Who is trying to make heiress Rachel Davenport think she's going crazy? And why? Former bad boy Seth Hammond will put his life—and his heart—on the line to find out.

#1433 TRIGGERED
Covert Cowboys, Inc.
Elle James
When ex-cop Ben Harding is hired to protect a woman and her child, he must learn to trust in himself and his abilities to defend truth and justice...and allow himself to love again.

#1434 FEARLESS
Corcoran Team
HelenKay Dimon
Undercover operative Davis Weeks lost everything when he picked work over his personal life. But now he gets a second chance when Lara Barton, the woman he's always loved, turns to him for help.

#1435 CARRIE'S PROTECTOR
Rebecca York
Carrie Mitchell is terrified to find herself in the middle of a terrorist plot...and in the arms of her tough-guy bodyguard, Wyatt Hawk.

#1436 FOR THE BABY'S SAKE
Beverly Long
Detective Sawyer Montgomery needs testimony from Liz Mayfield's pregnant teenage client, who is unexpectedly missing. Can Sawyer and Liz find the teen in time to save her and her baby?

You can find more information on upcoming Harlequin® titles, free excerpts and more at www.Harlequin.com.

HICNM0613

REQUEST YOUR FREE BOOKS!
2 FREE NOVELS PLUS 2 FREE GIFTS!

HARLEQUIN

INTRIGUE

BREATHTAKING ROMANTIC SUSPENSE

YES! Please send me 2 FREE Harlequin Intrigue® novels and my 2 FREE gifts (gifts are worth about $10). After receiving them, if I don't wish to receive any more books, I can return the shipping statement marked "cancel." If I don't cancel, I will receive 6 brand-new novels every month and be billed just $4.74 per book in the U.S. or $5.24 per book in Canada. That's a savings of at least 14% off the cover price! It's quite a bargain! Shipping and handling is just 50¢ per book in the U.S. and 75¢ per book in Canada.* I understand that accepting the 2 free books and gifts places me under no obligation to buy anything. I can always return a shipment and cancel at any time. Even if I never buy another book, the two free books and gifts are mine to keep forever.

182/382 HDN F42N

Name _____ (PLEASE PRINT)

Address _____ Apt. #

City _____ State/Prov. _____ Zip/Postal Code

Signature (if under 18, a parent or guardian must sign)

Mail to the **Harlequin® Reader Service:**
IN U.S.A.: P.O. Box 1867, Buffalo, NY 14240-1867
IN CANADA: P.O. Box 609, Fort Erie, Ontario L2A 5X3

**Are you a subscriber to Harlequin Intrigue books
and want to receive the larger-print edition?
Call 1-800-873-8635 or visit www.ReaderService.com.**

* Terms and prices subject to change without notice. Prices do not include applicable taxes. Sales tax applicable in N.Y. Canadian residents will be charged applicable taxes. Offer not valid in Quebec. This offer is limited to one order per household. Not valid for current subscribers to Harlequin Intrigue books. All orders subject to credit approval. Credit or debit balances in a customer's account(s) may be offset by any other outstanding balance owed by or to the customer. Please allow 4 to 6 weeks for delivery. Offer available while quantities last.

Your Privacy—The Harlequin® Reader Service is committed to protecting your privacy. Our Privacy Policy is available online at www.ReaderService.com or upon request from the Harlequin Reader Service.

We make a portion of our mailing list available to reputable third parties that offer products we believe may interest you. If you prefer that we not exchange your name with third parties, or if you wish to clarify or modify your communication preferences, please visit us at www.ReaderService.com/consumerschoice or write to us at Harlequin Reader Service Preference Service, P.O. Box 9062, Buffalo, NY 14269. Include your complete name and address.

HI13R

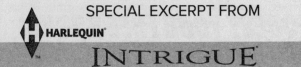
*When mysterious threats are made on the lives of
Kate Langsdon and her young daughter, only decorated
former Austin police officer Ben Harding is willing to
protect them at any cost.*

The warmth of his hands on her arms sent shivers throughout her body. "Really, it's fine," she said, even as she let him maneuver her to sit on the arm of the couch.

Ben squatted, pulled the tennis shoe off her foot and removed her sock. "I had training as a first responder on the Austin police force. Let me be the judge."

Kate held her breath as he lifted her foot and turned it to inspect the ankle, his fingers grazing over her skin.

"See? Just bumped it. It'll be fine in a minute." She cursed inwardly at her breathlessness. A man's hands on her ankle shouldn't send her into a tailspin. Ben Harding was a trained professional—touching a woman's ankle meant nothing other than a concern for health and safety. Nothing more.

Then why was she breathing like a teenager on her first date? Kate bent to slide her foot back into her shoe, biting hard on her lip to keep from crying out at the pain. When she turned toward him she could feel the warmth of his breath fan across her cheek.

"You should put a little ice on that," he said, his tone as smooth as warm syrup.

Ice was exactly what she needed. To chill her natural reaction to a handsome man, paid to help and protect her, not touch, hold or kiss her.

Kate jumped up and moved away from Ben and his gentle fingers. "I should get back outside. No telling what Lily is up to."

Ben caught her arm as she passed him. "You felt it, too, didn't you?"

Kate fought the urge to lean into him and sniff the musky scent of male. Four years was a long time to go without a man. "I don't know what you're talking about."

Ben held her arm a moment longer, then let go. "You're right. We should check on Lily."

Kate hurried for the door. Just as she crossed the threshold into the south Texas sunshine, a frightened scream made her racing heart stop.

Don't miss the dramatic conclusion to
TRIGGERED by Elle James.

Available July 2013, only from Harlequin Intrigue.